MORE RAVES FOR *JEMIMA SHORE AT THE SUNNY GRAVE:*
"For readers who like their murder British and civilized, their crime spiced with malice but not messy, this book—like Fraser's other works—won't disappoint."
—Dail Willis, Associated Press

"This compilation of short stories shows the true talents of Ms. Fraser as a mystery writer. The stories are diverse, never allowing the reader to become bored. She is creative, taking both male and female perspectives. Her characters work well with the easy-to-follow plots that have much irony and unexpected turns. A smooth writing style and a vibrant imagination have turned this collection of short stories into a potential classic."
—*Rendezvous*

"The stories abound with eccentric characters, taking twists and turns that cause chuckles in spite of their gruesomeness."
—*Dayton Daily News*

BY THE SAME AUTHOR

QUIET AS A NUN
THE WILD ISLAND
A SPLASH OF RED
COOL REPENTANCE
OXFORD BLOOD
YOUR ROYAL HOSTAGE
THE CAVALIER CASE
JEMIMA SHORE'S FIRST CASE AND OTHER STORIES

JEMIMA
SHORE
at the
SUNNY
GRAVE
AND OTHER STORIES

Antonia Fraser

CRIME LINE

BANTAM BOOKS
NEW YORK • TORONTO • LONDON • SYDNEY • AUCKLAND

JEMIMA SHORE AT THE SUNNY GRAVE
A Bantam Book / published by arrangement with the author

CRIME LINE and the portrayal of a boxed "cl" are trademarks of Bantam Books
a division of Bantam Doubleday Dell Publishing Group, Inc.

PUBLISHING HISTORY
Bloomsbury Publishing Ltd edition published 1991
Bantam hardcover edition / February 1993
Seal hardcover edition / February 1993
Bantam paperback / February 1994

ISBN 0-553-56498-6

Published simultaneously in the United States and Canada

PRINTED IN THE UNITED STATES OF AMERICA
RAD   0 9 8 7 6 5 4 3 2 1

For Mike Shaw
with much thanks
for the criminological encouragement

CONTENTS

AUTHOR'S NOTE

These stories first appeared in a variety of magazines and anthologies in England and the United States: *The Compleat Imbiber* edited by Cyril Ray; *Ellery Queen Mystery Magazine* edited by Eleanor Sullivan; *The John Creasey Collection* edited by Herbert Harris; the *London Evening News*; *Sisters in Crime* edited by Sara Paretsky; *Suntory Magazine*; *Winter's Crimes* edited by Hilary Hale; and *Woman's Realm*.

I am extremely grateful to all the editors who commissioned and published them.

1
JEMIMA SHORE
AT THE
SUNNY GRAVE

"This-is-your-graveyard-in-the-sun—"

The tall young man standing in her path was singing the words lightly but clearly. It took Jemima Shore a moment to realize exactly what message he was intoning to the tune of the famous calypso. Then she stepped back. It was a sinister and not particularly welcoming little parody.

> *This is my island in the sun*
> *Where my people have toiled since time*
>   *begun . . .*

Ever since she had arrived in the Caribbean, she seemed to have had the tune echoing in her ears. How old was it? How many years was it since the inimitable Harry Belafonte had first implanted it in everybody's consciousness? No matter. Whatever its age, the calypso was still being sung today with charm, vigour and a certain relentlessness on

Bow Island; and on the other West Indian islands she had visited in the course of her journey.

It was not the only tune to be heard of course. The loud noise of music, she had discovered, was an inseparable part of Caribbean life, starting with the airport. The heavy, irresistible beat of the steel band, the honeyed wail of the singers, all this was happening somewhere if not everywhere all over the islands late into the night: the joyous sound of freedom, of dancing, of drinking (rum punch) and, for the tourists at any rate, the sound of holiday.

It was not the sound of holiday for Jemima Shore, Investigator. Or not officially so. That was all to the good, Jemima being temperamentally one of those people whose best holidays combined some work with a good deal of pleasure. She could hardly believe it: Megalith Television, her employers, had actually agreed in principle to a programme which took her away from freezing Britain to the sunny Caribbean in late January. This was a reversal of normal practice, by which Cy Fredericks, Jemima's boss (and the effective boss of Megalith), was generally to be found relaxing in the Caribbean in February, while Jemima herself, if she got there at all, was liable to be dispatched into the inconvenient humidity of August. Not this time! And a fascinating project to boot. This was definitely her lucky year. Enlarging on the theme, she thought that Bow Island itself was probably going to be her lucky island . . .

"This is my island in the sun . . ." But that wasn't of course what the young man facing her had actually sung. "Your *graveyard* in the sun." Mine? Or yours? Since the man in question was standing between Jemima Shore and the historic grave she had come to visit, it was possible that he was being proprietorial as well as aggressive. On second thought, surely not. It was a joke, a cheerful joke on a cheerful, very sunny day. But the young man's expression was, it seemed to her, more threatening than quizzical.

Jemima gazed back with that special sweet smile so familiar to viewers of British television. (These same viewers were also aware from past experience that Jemima, sweet as her smile might be, stood no nonsense from anyone, at least not on her programme.)

On closer inspection, the man was not really as young as all that. She saw someone of perhaps roughly her own age—early thirties. He was white, although so deeply tanned that she guessed he was not a tourist but formed part of the small loyal European population of Bow Island, a place fiercely proud of its recent independence from a much larger neighbour.

The stranger's height, unlike his youth, was not an illusion; he towered over Jemima and she herself was not short; in fact, having long legs, she always surprised her television fans by how tall she was in real life. He was also handsome, or would have been except for an oddly formed, rather large nose with a high bridge to it and a pronounced aquiline curve. If the nose marred the regularity of his features, the impression left was not unattractive, in a man at least; it was not a nose that a woman could have easily carried off—an ordinary woman that is. The stranger was wearing whitish cotton shorts, like more or less every male on Bow Island, black or white. His orange T-shirt also bore the familiar island logo or crest: the outline of a bow in black, and a black hand drawing it back. Beneath the logo was printed one of the enormous variety of local slogans— cheerful again—designed to make a play upon the island's name. This one read: "THIS IS THE END OF THE SUN-BOW!"

No, in that friendly T-shirt, he was surely not intending to be aggressive.

In that case, the odd thing about the whole encounter

was that the stranger still stood absolutely still in Jemima's path. She could in fact glimpse the large stone Archer Tomb just behind him, which she recognized from the postcards. For a smallish place, Bow Island was indeed remarkably rich in historic relics. Nelson in his time had visited it with his fleet: like its neighbours, Bow Island had found itself engulfed in the Napoleonic Wars, faraway naval battles fought against an exotic West Indian background helping to decide the European contest. Two hundred-odd years before that, first British, then French, then British again had invaded and settled the islands, which had once belonged to Caribs and before that Arawaks: finally into this melting pot Africans had been brought forcibly to work the sugar plantations on which its wealth depended. All these elements in various degrees had gone to make up the people now known casually among themselves as the Bo'landers.

The Archer Tomb, the existence of which had in a sense brought Jemima across the Atlantic, belonged to the period of the second—and final—British settlement. Here was buried the most celebrated governor in Bow Island's history, Sir Valentine Archer. Even its name commemorated his long reign: Bow Island had originally been called by the name of a saint, and while it was true the island was vaguely formed in the shape of a bow, it was Governor Archer who had made the change: to signify ritually that this particular archer was in command of this particular bow.

Jemima knew that the monument, splendidly carved, would show Sir Valentine Archer himself with Isabella his wife beside him. This stone double bier was capped with a white wood structure reminiscent of a small church; it was either done to give the whole monument additional importance—although it must always have dominated the small churchyard by its sheer size—or to protect it from the weather. But Jemima had read that there were no Archer children inscribed on the tomb, contrary to seventeenth-century practice. This was because, as a local historian delicately put it, Governor Archer had been as a parent to the entire island . . . Or in the words of another purely local calypso:

> Across the sea came old Sir Valentine
> He came to be your daddy, and he came to be
> mine.

In short, no one monument could comprise the progeny of a man popularly supposed to have sired over a hundred children, legitimate and illegitimate. The legitimate line was, however, now on the point of dying out. It was to see Miss Isabella Archer, officially at least the last of her race, that Jemima Shore had come to the Caribbean. She hoped to make a programme about the old lady and her home, Archer Plantation House, alleged to be untouched in its decoration these fifty years. She wanted also to interview her generally about the changes Miss Archer had seen in her lifetime in this part of the world.

"Greg Harrison," said the man standing in Jemima's path suddenly. "And this is my sister Coralie." A girl who had been standing unnoticed by Jemima in the shade of the arched church porch stepped rather shyly forward. She was very brown, like her brother, and her blonde hair, whitened almost to flax by the sun, was pulled back into a ponytail. His sister: was there a resemblance? Coralie Harrison was wearing a similar orange T-shirt, but otherwise she was not much like her brother. She was quite short, for one thing, her features being appealing rather than beautiful; and—perhaps fortunately—she lacked her brother's commanding nose.

"Welcome to Bow Island, Miss Shore—" Coralie began. But her brother interrupted her. Ignoring his sister, he put out a hand, large, muscular and burnt to nut colour by the sun.

"I know why you're here and I don't like it," said Greg Harrison. "Stirring up forgotten things. Why don't you leave Miss Izzy to die in peace?" The contrast of the apparently friendly handshake and the hostile—if calmly spoken—words was disconcerting.

"I'm Jemima Shore." Obviously he knew that, but she did not, under the circumstances, add the word "Investigator." It was only how she was billed in her television series, after all, but might here give the wrong impression of a detective (as it sometimes did to the public at large). "Am I going to be allowed to inspect the Archer Tomb? Or is it to be across your dead body?" Jemima smiled again with sweetness; once more, experienced viewers might have recognized the expression as ominous.

"My dead body!" Greg Harrison smiled back in his turn. The effect, however, was not particularly warming. "Have you come armed to the teeth then?" Before she could answer, he began to hum the famous calypso again. Jemima imagined the words: "This is your graveyard in the sun." Then he added, "Might not be such a bad idea that, when you start to dig up things that should be buried." He gestured loosely round to the other lesser graves; but she doubted whether he had that kind of vandalism in mind.

Jemima decided it was time for vigorous action. Neatly side-stepping Greg Harrison, she marched firmly towards the Archer Tomb. There lay the carved couple. She read: "Sacred to the memory of Sir Valentine Archer, first Governor of this island, and his only wife Isabella, daughter of Randal Oxford, gentleman." She was reminded briefly of her favourite Philip Larkin poem about the Arundel Monument beginning "The Earl and Countess lie in stone . . ." and ending "All that remains of us is love."

But that couple lay a thousand miles away in the cloistered cool of Chichester Cathedral. Here the hot tropical sun burnt down on her naked head (she found she had taken off her large straw hat as a token of respect and quickly clapped it back on again). Here too there were palm trees among the graves instead of yews, their slender trunks bending like giraffes' necks in the breeze; in contrast to the very English-looking stone church with pointed Gothic windows beyond. She had once romantically laid white roses on the Arundel Monument; it was as the memory of the gesture returned to her that she spied the heap of bright pink and orange hibiscus blossoms lying on the stone before her. A shadow fell across it.

"Tina puts them there." Greg Harrison had followed her. "Every day she can manage it. Most days. Then she tells Miss Izzy what she's done. Touching, isn't it?" But he did not make it sound as if he found it especially touching. In fact there was so much bitterness, even malevolence, in his voice that for a moment, standing as she was in the sunny graveyard, Jemima felt quite chilled. "Or is it revolting?" he added; now the malevolence was quite naked.

"Greg," murmured Coralie Harrison faintly, as if in protest.

"Tina? That's Miss Archer's—Miss Izzy's—companion. We've corresponded. For the moment I can't remember her other name." She might as well see what was to be derived, of possible use in the programme, from this odd encounter.

"She's known as Tina Archer these days, I think you'll find. When she wrote to you, she probably signed the letter Tina Harrison." Greg Harrison looked at Jemima sardonically but she had genuinely forgotten the surname of the companion; it was after all not a particularly uncommon one.

"Greg! Darling." This time Coralie Harrison's voice was only just audible.

They were interrupted by a loud hail from the road: Jemima saw a young black man at the wheel of one of the convenient roofless Minis everyone seemed to drive around Bow Island. He stood up and started to shout something.

"Greg! Cora, you coming on to—" She missed the rest of it. Something about a boat and a fish. Coralie Harrison looked suddenly radiant, and for a moment even Greg Harrison actually looked properly pleased; he waved back.

"Hey, Joseph. Come and say hello to Miss Jemima Shore of BBC Television—"

"Megalith Television," Jemima interrupted, but in vain. Harrison continued. "You heard, Joseph. She's making a programme about Miss Izzy."

The man leapt gracefully out of the car and approached up the palm-lined path. Jemima saw that he too was extremely tall, like Greg Harrison. And like the vast majority of the Bo'landers she had so far met, he had the air of being a natural athlete. Whatever the genetic mix in the past of Carib and African and other things that had produced them, the Bo'landers were certainly wonderful looking. He kissed Coralie on both cheeks and patted her brother on the back.

"Miss Shore, meet Joseph—" But even before Greg Harrison had pronounced the surname, the mischievous expression had warned Jemima what it was likely to be. "Meet Joseph, Joseph Archer. Undoubtedly one of the ten thousand descendants of the philoprogenitive old gentleman at whose tomb you are so raptly gazing." All that remains of us is love, indeed, thought Jemima irreverently, as she shook Joseph Archer's hand; *pace* Larkin, it seemed that a good deal more remained of Sir Valentine than that . . .

"Oh, you'll find we're all called Archer round here," murmured Joseph pleasantly; unlike Greg Harrison he appeared to be genuinely welcoming. "As for Sir Val-en-tine," he pronounced it syllable by syllable like the calypso. "Don't pay too much attention to the stories. Otherwise how come we're not all living in that fine old Archer Plantation House?"

"Instead of merely my ex-wife. No, Coralie, don't protest. I could kill her for what she's doing." Jemima felt quite chilled by the extent of the violence in Greg Harrison's voice: he did not altogether sound as if he was joking on the subject of killing the former Mrs. Harrison. "Come, Joseph, we'll see about that fish of yours. Come on, Coralie." He strode off, unsmiling, accompanied by Joseph (who did smile). Coralie however tagged behind. She asked Jemima if there was anything she could do for her. Her manner was still shy but in her brother's absence a great deal more positively friendly. Jemima also had the impression quite strongly that Coralie Harrison wanted to communicate something to her, something she did not necessarily want her brother to hear.

"I could perhaps interpret, explain—" Coralie stopped. Jemima said nothing. "Certain things," went on Coralie with emphasis. "There are so many layers in a place like this. Just because it's small . . . An outsider doesn't always understand—"

"And I'm the outsider? Of course I am." Jemima had started to sketch the tomb for future reference, something for which she had a minor but useful talent. She forbore to observe truthfully if platitudinously that an outsider could also sometimes see local matters rather more clearly than those involved; she wanted to know what else Coralie Harrison had to say. Would she explain for example Greg's quite blatant dislike of his former wife?

But an impatient cry from her brother now in the car beside Joseph meant that Coralie for the time being had nothing more to add. She fled down the path. Jemima was left to ponder with renewed interest on her forthcoming visit to Miss Isabella Archer of Archer Plantation House. It was a visit which would include, she took it, a meeting with Miss Archer's companion who, like her employer, was currently dwelling in comfort there.

Comfort! Even from a distance, later that day, the square, low-built mansion had a comfortable air. More than that, it conveyed an impression of gracious and old-fashioned tranquillity. As Jemima drove her own rented sawn-off Mini up the long avenue of palm trees—much taller than those in the churchyard—she could fancy she was driving back in time to the days of Governor Archer, his copious banquets, parties and balls, all served by black slaves. For a moment the appearance of a young woman on the steps, with coffee-coloured skin and short black curly hair, did not disillusion her. However, unlike the maids in Jemima's own hotel who wore a pastiche of bygone servants' costumes at dinner—brightly coloured dresses to the ankle, white muslin aprons and turbans—this girl was wearing an up-to-the-minute scarlet halter top and cutaway shorts revealing most of her smooth brown legs. Old Sir Valentine, in public at any rate, would definitely not have approved.

Tina Archer: for so she introduced herself. It did not surprise Jemima Shore one bit to discover that Tina Archer—formerly Harrison—was easy to get on with. Anyone who abandoned the hostile and graceless Greg Harrison was already ahead in Jemima's book. But with Tina Archer chatting away at her side, so chic, even trendy in her appearance, the revelation of the interior of the house was in fact far more of a shock to her than it would otherwise have been. There was nothing, nothing at all of

the slightest modernity about it. Dust and cobwebs were
not literally there, perhaps, but in every other way, in its
gloom (so different from her own brightly painted hotel!),
its heavy wooden furniture (where were the light cane
chairs so suitable to the climate?), above all in its desola-
tion, Archer Plantation House reminded her of poor Miss
Havisham's time-warp home in *Great Expectations*.

And still worse, there was an atmosphere of sadness
hanging over the whole interior. Or perhaps it was mere
loneliness, a kind of sombre sterile grandeur which you felt
must stretch back centuries. All this was in violent contrast
to the sunshine still brilliant in the late afternoon, the
bushes of rioting brightly coloured tropical flowers outside.
None of this had Jemima expected. Information garnered in
London had led her to form quite a different picture of
Archer Plantation House, something far more like her
original impression of antique mellow grace, as she drove
down the avenue of palm trees.

It was just as Jemima was adapting to this surprise that
she discovered the figure of Miss Archer herself to be
equally astonishing. That is to say, having adjusted rapidly
from free and easy Tina to the mouldering sombre house,
she now had to adjust with equal rapidity all over again. For
on first inspection, the old lady—known by Jemima to be at
least 80—quickly banished all thoughts of Miss Havisham.
Here was no aged abandoned bride, forlorn in the decaying
wedding-dress of fifty years before.

Miss Izzy Archer was wearing a coolie straw hat, rather
similar to Jemima's own, but apparently tied under her chin
with a duster, a white loose man's shirt and faded blue jeans
cut off at the knee. On her feet were a pair of what looked
like a child's brown sandals. From the look of her she had
either just taken a shower wearing all this or had been
swimming. For Miss Izzy was dripping wet, making large

pools on the rich carpet and dark polished boards of the formal drawing-room, all dark red brocade and swagged fringed curtains, where she had received Jemima. It was possible to see this even in the filtered light seeping through the heavy brown shutters which shut out the view of the sea.

"Oh, don't fuss so, Tina dear," exclaimed Miss Izzy impatiently (although Tina had in fact said nothing). "What do a few drops of water matter? Stains? What stains?" (Tina still had not spoken.) "Let the government put it right when the time comes." Although Tina Archer continued to be silent, gazing amiably, even cheerfully, at her employer, nevertheless in some way she stiffened, froze in her polite listening attitude. Instinctively Jemima knew that she was in some way put out or upset.

"Now, don't be silly, Tina, don't take on, dear," rattled on the old lady, now shaking herself free of water like a small but stout dog. "You know what I mean. If you don't, who does, since half the time I don't know what I mean, let alone what I say? You can put it all right one day; is that better? After all, you'll have plenty of money to do it. You can afford a few new covers and carpets." So saying, Miss Izzy, taking Jemima by the hand and attended by the still silent Tina, led the way to the furthest dark red sofa. Looking remarkably wet from top to toe, she sat down firmly right in the middle of it.

It was in this way that Jemima Shore first realized that Archer Plantation House would not necessarily pass to the newly independent government of Bow Island on its owner's death. Miss Izzy, if she had her way, was intending to leave it all, house and fortune, to Tina. Among other things, this meant that Jemima was no longer making a programme about a house destined shortly to be a national museum. Which was very much part of the arrangement which had brought her to the island and had incidentally secured the friendly cooperation of that same new government. Was all this new? How new? Did the new government know? If the will had been signed, they must know . . .

"I've signed the will this morning, dear," Miss Archer pronounced triumphantly; she had an uncanny ability to answer unspoken questions. "Then I went swimming to celebrate. I always celebrate things with a good swim. So much more healthy than rum—or champagne. Although there's still plenty of *that* in the cellar." She paused. "So there you are, aren't you, dear. Or there you will be. Here you will be. Thompson says there'll be trouble of course. What can you expect these days? Everything is trouble since independence—not that I'm against independence. Far from it. But everything new brings new trouble here, in addition to all the old troubles, so that the troubles get more and more. On Bow Island no troubles ever go away. Why is that?" But Miss Izzy did not stop for an answer.

"No, I'm all for independence and I shall tell you all about that, my dear"—she turned to Jemima and put one damp hand on her sleeve—"on your programme. I'm being a Bo'lander born and bred, you know." It was true that Miss Izzy, unlike Tina for example, spoke with the peculiar, slightly sing-song intonation of the islanders: not unattractive to Jemima's ears.

"I was born in this very house eighty-two years ago in April," went on Miss Izzy. "You shall come to my birthday party—I was born during a hurricane! A good start! But my mother died in childbirth, you know, they should never have got in that new-fangled doctor, just because he came from England, a total fool he was, I remember him well. They should have had a good Bo'lander midwife, old Eloise from Sugar Horse Bay knew everything about having babies, then my mother wouldn't have died, my father would have had sons—"

Miss Izzy was drifting away into a host of reminiscences; while these were supposed to be what Jemima had come to hear, her thoughts were actually racing off in quite a different direction. Trouble? What trouble? Where did Greg Harrison for example stand in all this—Greg Harrison who wanted Miss Izzy to be left to "die in peace?" Greg Harrison who had been married to Tina and was no longer. And what of Tina Archer, now an heiress to a fortune?

Above all, why was this forthright old lady intending to leave everything to her companion? For one thing, Jemima did not know how seriously to treat the matter of Tina's surname. Joseph Archer had laughed off the whole subject of Sir Valentine's innumerable descendants. But perhaps Tina Archer was in some special way connected to Miss Izzy. Looking at the beautiful coffee-coloured Tina, Jemima thought she might be the product of some rather more recent union between a rakish Archer and a Bo'lander maiden; more recent than the seventeenth century, that is.

Her attention was wrenched back to Miss Izzy's reminiscing monologue by the mention of the Archer Tomb.

"You've seen the grave? You saw it this morning. Tina there has discovered that it's all a fraud. A great big lie, lying under the sun—yes, Tina dear, you once said that. Sir Valentine Archer, my great, great, great"—an infinite number of greats followed before Miss Izzy finally pronounced the word grandfather, but Jemima had to admit that she did seem to be counting. "He had a great big lie perpetuated on his tombstone."

"What Miss Izzy means, you know—" This was the first time Tina Archer had spoken since they entered the darkened drawing-room; she was still standing while Jemima and Miss Izzy sat. Perhaps there had been some wisdom in her silence. For Miss Izzy immediately interrupted her.

"Don't tell me what I mean, child," rapped out the old lady; her tone was imperious rather than indulgent. Tina might for a moment have been a plantation worker two hundred years earlier than an independent-minded girl in the late twentieth century. "It's the inscription which is a lie. She wasn't his only wife." Miss Izzy quoted: "'His only wife, Isabella, daughter of Randal Oxford, gentleman.'" The very inscription should have warned us. Tina wants to see justice done to poor little Lucie Anne and so do I. Independence indeed! I've been independent all my life and I'm certainly not stopping now. Tell me, Miss Shore, you're a clever young woman from television; you know the answer to this question. Why do you bother to contradict something unless it's true all along? That's the way you work all the time in television, don't you?"

Jemima was wondering just how to answer this question diplomatically without necessarily traducing her profession when Tina Archer firmly, and this time successfully, took over from her employer.

"I read history at university in the UK, Jemima. Genealogical research is my speciality. I was helping Miss Izzy put her papers in order for the museum—or what was to be the museum. Then the request came for your programme. I began to dig a little deeper. That's how I found the marriage certificate. Old Sir Valentine *did* marry his young Carib mistress, known as Lucie Anne. Late in life: long after his first wife died. That's Lucie Anne who was the mother of his two youngest children. He was getting old and for some reason he decided to marry her: the Church, maybe. In its way this has always been a God-fearing island; perhaps Lucie Anne, who was very young and very beautiful, put pressure on the old man via the Church. At any rate these last two children, of all the hundreds he sired, would have been legitimate."

"And so?" questioned Jemima in her most encouraging manner.

"I'm descended from Lucie Anne—and Sir Valentine of course." Tina returned sweet smile for smile. "I've traced that too from the church records, baptisms, marriages and so forth. Again not too difficult, given the strength of the Church here. Not too difficult for an expert, at all events. Oh, I've got all sorts of blood, like most of us round here, including a Spanish grandmother and maybe some French blood too. But the Archer descent is perfectly straightforward and clear."

Tina seemed aware that Jemima Shore was gazing at her with new respect; did she however understand the actual tenor of Jemima's thoughts? "This is a formidable person," Jemima was reflecting. "Charming, yes, but formidable. And ruthless. Yes, maybe that too on occasion." Jemima was also, to be frank, wondering just how she was going to present this sudden change of angle in her programme on Megalith Television. On the one hand it might now be seen as a romantic rags-to-riches story, the discovery of the lost heiress. On the other hand, just supposing Tina Archer was not so much an heiress as an adventuress? In that case what would Megalith—what did Jemima Shore—make of a bright young woman putting across a load of false history on an innocent old lady? In those circumstances she could understand how the man by the sunny grave might display his contempt for Tina Archer.

"I met Greg Harrison by the Archer Tomb this morning." Jemima threw the comment in deliberately to gauge Tina's reaction. "Your ex-husband, I take it?"

"Of course he's her ex-husband." It was Miss Izzy who chose to answer. "That no-good. Gregory Harrison has been a no-good since the day he was born. And that sister of his. Drifters. Not one job between them. Sailing. Fishing. As if the world owed them a living."

"Half-sister. Coralie is his half-sister. And she works in a hotel boutique." Tina spoke perfectly equably but once again Jemima guessed that she was in some way put out. "Greg is the no-good in that family." For all her calm, there was a hint of suppressed anger in her references to her former husband; with what bitterness that marriage must have ended.

"No-good the pair of them. You're well out of that marriage, Tina dear," exclaimed Miss Izzy. Once again Tina, following her elaborate explanation of her own place in Archer history, relapsed into silence. "And do sit down, child. You're standing there like some kind of housekeeper. And where is Hazel anyway? It's nearly half-past five. It'll begin to get dark soon. We might go down to the terrace and watch the sun sink. Where is Hazel, and Henry too? He ought to be bringing up some punch. Now the Archer Plantation punch, Miss Shore—wait till you taste it, one secret ingredient—my father always said—"

Miss Izzy was happily returning to the past.

"I'll get the punch. Didn't you say Hazel could have the day off? Her sister is getting married over at Tamarind Creek. Henry has taken her."

"Then where's the boy? Where's what's-his-name? Little Joseph." The old lady was beginning to sound quite petulant.

"There isn't a boy any longer," explained Tina patiently. "Just Hazel and Henry. And as for Joseph—well, little Joseph Archer is quite grown up now, isn't he?"

"Of course he is! I didn't mean that Joseph. He came to see me the other day. Wasn't there another boy called Joseph? Perhaps that was before the war. My father had a stable boy—"

"I'll get the rum punch." Tina vanished swiftly and gracefully.

"Pretty creature!" murmured Miss Izzy after her. "Archer blood. It always shows. They do say the best-looking Bo'landers are still called Archer." But when Tina returned the old lady's mood had changed again.

"I'm cold and damp," she declared. "I might get a chill sitting here. And soon I'm going to be all alone in the house. I hate being left alone. Ever since I was a little girl, I've hated being alone, everyone knows little Miss Isabella mustn't be left alone. Tina, you have to stay to dinner. Miss Shore, you have to stay too. It's so lonely here by the sea. What happens if someone breaks in? Don't frown. Plenty of bad people about. That's one thing which hasn't got better since independence. Hazel was telling me about that robbery—"

"Of course I'm staying," replied Tina easily. "I've arranged it with Hazel." Jemima was wondering guiltily if she too ought to stay. But it was the night of her hotel's regular party on the beach: barbecue followed by dancing to a steel band. Jemima, who loved to dance in the northern hemisphere, was longing equally to try out the southern experience. Dancing under the stars by the sea sounded idyllic. Did Miss Izzy really need extra company?

Her eyes met those of Tina Archer across the old lady's straw-hatted head. Tina shook her head slightly. Her lips framed the words: "No need." After a sip of the famous rum punch—whatever the secret ingredient, it was the strongest she had yet tasted on the island—Jemima was able to make her escape. In any case the punch was having a manifestly relaxing effect on Miss Izzy herself; she became rapidly quite tipsy. Jemima wondered how long she would actually stay awake. The next time they met must be in the freshness of a morning.

Jemima drove away just as the enormous red sun was rushing down below the horizon. The beat of the waves from the shore pursued her. Actually Archer Plantation House was set in quite a lonely position on its own spit of land at the end of its own long avenue; she could hardly blame Miss Izzy for not wanting to be abandoned there. Jemima listened to the sound of the waves until the very different noise of the steel band in the next village along the shore took over. That noise transferred Jemima Shore's thoughts temporarily from recent events at Archer Plantation House to the prospect of her evening ahead. One way or another, for a brief space of time, she stopped thinking altogether about Miss Isabella Archer.

That was because the beach party was at first exactly what Jemima had expected: relaxed, good-natured and noisy. She found her cares gradually floating away as she danced and danced again, with a series of partners, English, American and Bo'lander, to the beat of the steel band. That rum punch of Miss Izzy's—with its secret ingredient—must have been lethal because its effects seemed to stay with her for hours. She decided she did not even need the generous profferings of the hotel mixture (a good deal weaker than Miss Izzy's beneath its lavish surface scattering of nutmeg). Others however decided that the hotel rum punch was exactly what they did need. All in all it was already a very good party long before the sliver of the new moon became visible as it rose over the now black waters of the Caribbean. Jemima, temporarily alone, tilted back her head as she stood by the lapping waves at the edge of the beach and fixed the moon in her sights.

"You going to wish on that new little moon?" She turned. A tall man—at least a head taller than she was—was standing beside her on the sand; she had not heard him come up to her, even the gentle noise of the waves masking his approach. For a moment she did not recognize Joseph Archer in his loose flowered shirt and long white trousers;

so different did he look from the fisherman encountered that noon at the graveside.

In this way it came about that the second part of the beach party was quite unexpected, at least from Jemima Shore's point of view.

"I ought to wish. I ought to wish to make a good programme, I suppose. That would be a good professional thing to do."

"Miss Izzy Archer and all that?"

"Miss Izzy, Archer Plantation House, Bow Island, to say nothing of the Archer Tomb, old Sir Valentine and all that. Quite a lot to discuss really." She decided not to mention Tina Archer—and all that—for the time being.

"All that!" He sighed. Then he said, "Listen, Jemima, it's good this band. We're saying it's about the best on the island these days. Let's be dancing, shall we? Then you and me can talk about all that in the morning. In my office, you know."

It was the distinct authority with which Joseph Archer spoke, quite as much as the mention of his office, which intrigued Jemima. Before she lost herself still further in the rhythm of the dance—which she had a feeling that, with Joseph Archer to help her, she was about to do—she must find out just what he meant. And for that matter, just who he was.

The second question was easily answered; it also provided the answer to the first. Joseph Archer might or might not go fishing from time to time when he was off-duty; but he was also a member of the newly formed Bo'lander government. Quite an important one in fact. Quite important in the eyes of the world in general, and particularly important in the eyes of Jemima Shore, Investigator. For Joseph Archer was the minister dealing with tourism, his brief extending to such matters as conservation, the Bo'lander historic heritage and—as he described it to her—"the future National Archer Plantation House Museum."

Once again it did not seem the appropriate moment to mention Tina Archer and *her* possible future ownership of the plantation house. As Joseph himself had said, the morning would do for all that. In his office in Bowtown. They danced on for a while. It was as Jemima had suspected it would be: something to lose herself in, perhaps dangerously so. "This is my island in the sun": that tune too was played and Jemima never once heard the graveyard words in her imagination.

Then Joseph Archer, most politely and apparently regretfully, said he had to leave, an extremely early appointment, and not with a fish either, he added with a smile. Jemima felt a pang which she hoped did not show. But there was plenty of time, wasn't there? There would be other nights, and other parties, perhaps more intimate, other nights on the beach as the moon waxed to full in the two weeks she had before she must return to England.

Jemima's personal party stopped but the rest of the celebration went on late into the night, spilling on to the sands, even into the sea, long after the sliver of the moon had vanished. Jemima, sleeping fitfully, heard the noise in the distance. She was visited by dreams in which Joseph Archer, Tina and Miss Izzy executed some kind of elaborate dance not at all like the kind of island jump-up she had recently been enjoying.

Far away on Archer Plantation's lonely peninsula the peace was broken not by a steel band but by the rough sound of the waves bashing against the rocks at its furthest point. A stranger might have been surprised to see that the lights were still on in the great drawing-room, the shutters having been drawn back once the sun was gone: but nobody born on Bow Island, a fisherman out to sea for example, would have found that at all odd. Everyone knew that Miss Izzy Archer was frightened of the dark and liked to go to bed with all her lights blazing. Especially when Hazel had gone to her sister's wedding and Henry had taken her there; another fact of island life which most Bo'landers would have known.

In her room overlooking the sea, tossing in the big four-poster bed in which she had been born over eighty years ago, Miss Izzy, like Jemima Shore, slept fitfully. After a while she got out of bed and went to one of the long windows. Jemima would have found her night clothes, like her swimming costume, bizarre: for Miss Izzy was not wearing the kind of formal Victorian nightdress which might have gone with the house; rather she was "using up," as she quaintly put it, her father's ancient burgundy silk pyjamas, purchased so many aeons ago in Jermyn Street. As the late Sir John Archer, Baronet, had been several feet taller than his plump little daughter, the long trouser legs trailed on the floor behind her.

Miss Izzy continued to stare out of the window. Her gaze followed the direction of the terrace which led in a series of parterres, once grandly planted, now overgrown, down to the rocks and the sea. Although the waters themselves were mostly blackness, the Caribbean night was not entirely dark; besides, the light from the drawing-room windows streamed out on to the nearest terrace. Miss Izzy rubbed her eyes, then looked away. She turned back into the bedroom where the celebrated oil painting of old Sir Valentine, hanging over the mantelpiece, dominated the room. Rather confusedly—she was confused, she must have drunk far too much of that punch—she decided that her ancestor was trying to encourage her to be valiant in the face of danger for the first time in her life. She, little Isabella Archer, spoilt and petted Izzy, his last legitimate descendant, no, not his last legitimate descendant, still, the habits of a lifetime were difficult to break, she was being spurred on to something courageous by the hawk-like gaze of the fierce autocrat.

"But I'm so old—" thought Miss Izzy; then, "But not *too* old. Once you let people know you're not after all a coward—"

She looked out of the window once more. The effects of the punch were wearing off. Now she was quite certain of what she was seeing. Something dark, darkly clad, dark-skinned, what did it matter, someone dark had come out of the sea, and was now proceeding silently in the direction of the house.

"I must be brave," thought Miss Izzy. She said aloud, "Then he'll be proud of me. His brave girl." Whose brave girl? No, not Sir Valentine's, Daddy's brave girl. Her thoughts began to float away again into the past. "I wonder if Daddy will take me on a swim with him to celebrate?"

Miss Izzy started to go downstairs. She had just reached the door of the drawing-room and was standing looking into the decaying red velvet interior, still brightly illuminated, at the moment when the black-clad intruder stepped into the room through the open window.

Even before the intruder began to move slowly towards her—dark-gloved hands outstretched—Miss Izzy Archer knew without doubt in her rapidly beating old heart that Archer Plantation, the house in which she had been born, was also the house in which she was about to die.

"Miss Izzy Archer is dead. Some person went and killed her last night. A robber maybe." It was Joseph Archer who broke the news to Jemima Shore the next morning.

He spoke across the broad desk of his formal office in Bowtown. Joseph Archer's voice was hollow, distant, only the familiar Bo'lander sing-song to connect him with Jemima's handsome dancing partner of the night before. In his short-sleeved but official-looking white shirt and dark trousers he looked once again completely different from the cheerful ragged fisherman Jemima had first encountered. This was indeed the rising young Bo'lander politician she was seeing: a member of the newly formed government of Bow Island. Even the tragic fact of the death—the murder as it seemed—of an old lady seemed to strike no chord of emotion in him.

Then Jemima looked again and saw what looked suspiciously like tears in Joseph Archer's eyes.

"I just heard myself, you know. The Chief of Police, Sandy Marlow, is my cousin." He did not attempt to brush away the tears. If that was what they were. But the words were presumably meant as an explanation. Of what? Of shock? Grief? Shock he must surely have experienced, but grief? Jemima decided at this point that she could at least enquire delicately about Joseph Archer's precise relationship to Miss Izzy. It came back to her that he had visited the old lady the week previously, if Miss Izzy's rather vague words concerning "Little Joseph" were to be trusted. She was thinking not so much of a possible blood relationship as some other kind of connection. After all Joseph Archer himself had dismissed the former idea in the graveyard. His words about Sir Valentine and his numerous progeny came back to her: "Don't pay too much attention to the stories. Otherwise how come we're not all living in that fine old Archer Plantation House?" At which point Greg Harrison had commented with obvious fury, "Instead of just my ex-wife." The exchange made far more sense to her of course, now that she knew of the position of Tina Harrison, now Tina Archer, in Miss Izzy's will.

The will! Tina Archer would now inherit! And she would inherit in the light of a will signed that very morning, the morning of the day of Miss Izzy's death. Clearly Joseph had been correct when he dismissed the claim of the many Bo'landers called Archer to be descended in any meaningful fashion from Sir Valentine. There was already a considerable difference between Tina, the allegedly sole legitimate descendant (other than Miss Izzy), and the rest of the Bo'lander Archers. In the future, with Tina come into her inheritance, the gap would widen even more.

It was extremely hot in Joseph Archer's office; there was no air-conditioning. It was not so much that Bow Island was an unsophisticated place as that the persistent breeze on the island made it generally unnecessary. The North American tourists who were beginning to request air-conditioning in the hotels, reflected Jemima, would only succeed in ruining the most perfect kind of natural ventilation. But a government office in Bowtown was rather different. A huge fan in the ceiling made the papers on Joseph Archer's desk stir uneasily. Jemima felt a ribbon of sweat trickle down beneath her long, loose white T-shirt, which she had belted as a dress to provide some kind of formal attire in which to call on a Bo'lander minister in working hours.

By this time Jemima's disbelieving numbness on the subject of Miss Izzy's death, no, her *murder*, for heaven's sake, was wearing off. She was struck by the frightful poignancy of that last encounter in the decaying grandeur of Archer Plantation House: worse still, the old lady's pathetic fear of loneliness was beginning to haunt her. Miss Izzy had been so passionate in her determination not to be abandoned: "Everyone knows little Miss Isabella mustn't be left . . . It's so lonely here by the sea. What happens if someone breaks in?"

Well, someone had broken in. Or so it was presumed. Joseph Archer's words: "A robber maybe." And this robber—maybe—had killed the old lady in the process.

Jemima began hesitantly, "I'm so sorry, Joseph. What a ghastly tragedy! You knew her? Well, I suppose everyone round here must have known her—"

"All the days of my life, since I was a little boy. My mamma was one of her maids, just a little thing herself, and then she died. She's in that churchyard, you know, in a corner. Miss Izzy was very good to me when my mamma died, kind, oh yes. She was kind. Now you'd think that independence, *our* independence, would be hard for an old lady like her, but Miss Izzy she just liked it very much. 'England's no good to me any more, Joseph,' she said. 'I'm a Bo'lander just like the rest of you.'"

"You saw her—last week, I believe. Miss Izzy told me that herself."

Joseph Archer gazed at Jemima steadily; the emotion had vanished. "I went to talk with her, yes. She had some foolish idea of changing her mind about things. Just a fancy, you know. But that's over. May she rest in peace, little old Miss Izzy. We'll have our National Museum now, that's for sure, and we'll remember her with it. It'll make a good museum for our history. Didn't they tell you in London, Jemima?" There was pride in Joseph Archer's voice as he concluded, "Miss Izzy Archer has left everything in her will to the people of Bow Island."

Jemima swallowed hard. Was it true? Or rather, was it still true? Had Miss Izzy really signed a new will yesterday? She had been quite circumstantial on the subject, mentioning someone called Thompson, her lawyer no doubt, who thought there would be "trouble" as a result.

"Joseph," she said, "Tina Archer was there too yesterday afternoon, up at Archer Plantation House."

"Oh, that girl, that sweet Tina oh, the trouble she made, tried to make. Tina and her stories and her fine education and her history. And she's so pretty!" Joseph's tone was momentarily quite violent but he finished more calmly. "The police are waiting at the hospital, you know. She's not speaking yet, she's not even conscious." Then even more calmly, "Maybe she's not so pretty now. That robber beat her, you see."

It was hotter than ever in the Bowtown office and even the papers on the desk were hardly stirring in the waft of the fan. Jemima saw Joseph's face swimming before her. She absolutely must not faint: she never fainted. Jemima concentrated desperately on what Joseph Archer was telling her, the picture he was re-creating of the night of the murder. The shock of learning that Tina Archer had also been present in the house when Miss Izzy was killed was irrational: she realized that. Hadn't Tina promised the old lady to stay with her?

Joseph was telling her that Miss Izzy's body had been found in the drawing-room by the cook Hazel, returning from her sister's wedding at first light. It was a grisly touch that because Miss Izzy was wearing red silk pyjamas ("her Daddy's"), and all the furnishings of the drawing-room were dark red as well, poor Hazel had not at first realized the extent of her mistress's injuries: the blood which was everywhere as her little body lay slumped in the centre of the room. Not only was there blood everywhere, there was water too, pools of it. Whatever—whoever it was had killed Miss Izzy had come out of the sea. Wearing rubber shoes—or flippers—and probably gloves as well.

A moment later Hazel was in no doubt about what had hit Miss Izzy. The club, still stained with blood, had been left lying on the floor of the hall (the cook, deposited by Henry, had originally entered by the kitchen door). The club, although not of Bo'lander manufacture, belonged to the house: it was a relic, African probably, of Sir John Archer's travels in other parts of the former British Empire, and hung heavy and short-handled on the drawing-room wall. Possibly Sir John had in mind to wield it against unlawful intruders; to Miss Izzy it had been simply one more family memento. She never touched it. Now it had killed her.

"No prints anywhere. So far. That's what Sandy Marlow told me."

"And Tina?" asked Jemima with dry lips; the idea of the pools of water stagnant on the floor of the drawing-room mingled with Miss Izzy's blood reminded her only too vividly of the old lady when last seen: soaking wet in her bizarre swimming costume of shirt and shorts, defiantly sitting down on her own sofa.

"The robber ransacked the house. Even the cellar—the champagne cases Miss Izzy boasted about must have been too heavy, though. He drank some rum. The police don't know yet just what he took—silver snuff-boxes maybe, plenty of those about. Hazel hated to clean them." Joseph sighed. "Then he went upstairs."

"And found Tina Archer?"

"In one of the bedrooms. He didn't hit her with the same weapon—lucky for her—as he'd have killed her just like he killed Miss Izzy. Left it downstairs and picked up something a good deal lighter. Probably didn't reckon seeing her or anyone there at all. Thought the house would be quite empty with Hazel going away. 'Cept for Miss Izzy that is. She must have surprised him. Maybe she woke up: robbers— well, our island is a good place, Jemima, even if like everywhere in the whole wide world it holds some bad people too. All I can say is that robbers here don't generally go and kill people unless they're frightened."

Without warning Joseph Archer slumped down in front of her and put his head in his hands. He murmured something like, "When we find him, who did it to Miss Izzy—"

It was not until the next day that Tina Archer was able to speak even haltingly to the police. Like most of the rest of the Bow Island population, Jemima Shore was informed of the fact almost immediately. Claudette, manageress of her hotel, a sympathetic if loquacious character, just happened to have a niece who was a nurse . . . but that was the way information always spread about the island, no need for newspapers or radio. This private telegraph was far more efficient.

Jemima had spent the intervening twenty-four hours swimming rather aimlessly, sunbathing and making little tours of the island in her Mini. She was wondering at what point she should inform Megalith Television of the brutal way in which her projected programme had been terminated and make arrangements to return to London. After a bit the investigative instinct, that inveterate curiosity which would not be stilled, came to the fore: she found she was speculating all the time about Miss Izzy's death. A robber—maybe? A robber who had also tried to kill Tina Archer? Or a robber who had merely been surprised by her presence in the house? What connection if any had all this with Miss Izzy's will?

The will again: but that was one thing Jemima did not have to speculate about for very long. For Claudette the manageress also just happened to be married to the brother of Hazel, Miss Izzy's cook . . . In this way Jemima was apprised—along with the rest of Bow Island no doubt—that Miss Izzy had indeed signed a new will down in Bowtown on the morning of her death. That Eddy Thompson, the solicitor, had begged her not to do it, that Miss Izzy had done it, that Miss Izzy had still looked after Hazel all right as she had promised (and Henry who had worked for her even longer), and some jewellery would go to a cousin in England ("seeing as Miss Izzy's mother's jewels were in an English bank anyway since long back"), but for the rest . . . Well, there would be no National Bo'lander Museum now. That was for sure. Everything else, that fine old Archer Plantation House, Miss Izzy's fortune—reputedly enormous but who knew for sure?—everything else would go to Tina Archer.

If she recovered, of course. But the latest cautious bulletin from Claudette via the niece-who-was-a-nurse, confirmed by a few other loquacious people on the island, was that Tina Archer *was* recovering. Slowly. The police had already been able to interview her. In a few days time she would be able to leave the hospital. She was determined, quite determined, to attend Miss Izzy's funeral, which would be held, naturally enough, in that little English-looking church with its incongruous tropical vegetation overlooking the sunny grave. For Miss Izzy had long ago made clear her own determination to be buried in the Archer Tomb, along with Governor Sir Valentine and "his only wife Isabella."

"As the last of the Archers. But she had to get permission since it's a national monument. And of course the government couldn't do enough for her. So they gave it. Then. Ironic, isn't it?" The speaker making absolutely no attempt to conceal her own disgust was Coralie Harrison. "And now we learn that she wasn't the last of the Archers. Not even officially. And we shall have the so-called Miss Tina Archer as chief mourner. And while the Bo'lander government desperately looks for ways to get round the will and grab the house for their precious museum, nobody quite has the bad taste to go ahead and say: no, no burial in the Archer Tomb for naughty old Miss Izzy. Since she hasn't after all left the people of Bow Island a penny."

"It should be an interesting occasion," Jemima interrupted. She was sitting with Coralie Harrison under the conical thatched roof of the hotel's beach bar. This was where she first danced, then sat out with Joseph Archer on the night of the new moon—the night Miss Izzy had been killed. Now the sea sparkled under the sun as though there were crystals scattered on its surface; today there were no waves at all and the happy water-skiers crossed and recrossed the wide bay with its palm-fringed shore. Enormous brown pelicans perched on some stakes which indicated where rocks lay. Every now and then one would take off like an unwieldy aeroplane and fly slowly and inquisitively over the heads of the swimmers. It was a tranquil, even an idyllic scene. But somewhere in the distant peninsula lay Archer Plantation House, not only shuttered but now, she imagined, also sealed up by the police.

Coralie Harrison had sauntered up to the bar from the beach. She traversed the few yards with seeming casualness. All Bo'landers frequently exercised their right to promenade along the sands unchecked (as in most Caribbean islands, no one owned any portion of the beach in Bow Island, even outside the most stately mansion like Archer Plantation House—except the people). Jemima however was in no doubt that this was a planned visit. She had not forgotten that first meeting, and Coralie's tentative approach to her, interrupted by Greg's peremptory cry.

It was the day after the inquest on Miss Izzy's death. Her body had been released by the police and the funeral would soon follow. Jemima admitted to herself that she was interested enough in the whole Archer family—in its various branches—to want to attend it, quite apart from the tenderness for the old lady herself, based on that brief meeting. To Megalith Television, in a telex from Bowtown, she had spoken merely of tying up a few loose ends resulting from the cancellation of her programme.

There had been an open verdict at the inquest. Tina Archer's evidence in the shape of a sworn statement had not really contributed much which was not known or suspected already. She had been asleep upstairs in one of the many fairly derelict bedrooms kept ostensibly ready for guests. The bedroom chosen for her by Miss Izzy had however not faced on to the sea; the chintz curtains in this back room, bearing some dated rosy pattern from a remote era, were not quite so bleached and tattered as elsewhere, since they had been protected from the sun and salt.

Miss Izzy had gone to bed in good spirits, reassured by the fact that Tina Archer was going to spend the night. She had drunk several more rum punches and had offered to have Henry fetch some of her father's celebrated champagne from the cellar. As a matter of fact Miss Izzy often made this offer after a few draughts of punch; she was reminded by Tina that Henry was away and the subject was dropped.

Tina Archer in her statement said that she had no clue as to what might have woken the old lady and induced her to descend the stairs; it was right out of character in her own opinion. Miss Isabella Archer was a lady of independent mind but notoriously frightened of the dark, hence Tina's presence at the house in the first place. As to her own recollection of the attack, Tina had so far managed to dredge very few of the details from her memory: the blow to the back of the head had—whether temporarily or permanently—expunged all the immediate circumstances from her consciousness. She had a vague idea that there had been a bright light, but even that was rather confused and might be part of the blow she had suffered. Basically Tina Archer could remember nothing between going to bed in the tattered rose-patterned four-poster and waking up in hospital.

Coralie's lip trembled. She bowed her head and sipped at her long drink through a straw: both Coralie and Jemima were drinking some exotic mixture of fruit juice—alcohol-free—invented by Matthew the barman (not a relation of Claudette's for once, being from Antigua). There was a wonderful soft breeze coming in from the sea and Coralie was dressed in a loose flowered cotton dress: but she looked hot and angry. "Tina schemed for everything all her life and now she's got it. That's what I wanted to warn you about that morning in the churchyard—don't trust Tina Archer, I wanted to say. Now it's too late: she's got it all. When she was married to Greg I tried to like her, Jemima, honestly I did. Little Tina Archer, so cute and yet so clever, but always trouble—"

"Joseph Archer feels rather the same way about her, I gather." Was it her imagination or did Coralie's face soften slightly at the sound of Joseph's name?

"Does he now? I'm glad. He fancied her too once upon a time, long ago. Well, she is quite pretty." Their eyes met. "Not all that pretty, but if you like the type—" Jemima and Coralie both laughed. The fact was that Coralie Harrison was quite appealing—if you liked her type—but Tina Archer was ravishing by any standards. All the time Jemima was wondering exactly what it was that Coralie, beneath the complaints, had come to say.

"Greg absolutely loathes her now, of course," Coralie continued, firmly. "Especially since he heard the news about the will. When we met you that morning up at the church he'd just been told. Hence, well, I'm sorry, but he was very rude, wasn't he? I wanted to apologize for that, explain."

"More hostile than rude." But Jemima had begun to work out the timing. "You mean, your brother knew about the will *before* Miss Izzy was killed?" she exclaimed.

"Oh yes. Someone from Eddy Thompson's office told Greg: Daisy Marlow maybe, he takes her out. Of course we all knew it was on the cards, except we hoped Joseph had argued Miss Izzy out of it. And he *would* have argued her out of it—given time. That museum is everything to Joseph."

"Your brother and Miss Izzy—that wasn't an easy relationship, I gather?" Jemima thought she was using her gentlest and most persuasive interviewer's voice.

But Coralie countered with something like defiance. "You sound like the police!"

"Why, have they—?"

"Well of course they have." Coralie answered the question even before Jemima had completed it. "Everyone knows that Greg absolutely hated Miss Izzy, blamed her for breaking up his marriage, for taking little Tina and giving her ideas."

"Wasn't it rather the other way round? Tina delving into the family records for the museum and then my programme. You said *she* was such a schemer." Jemima wondered if she was beginning to see some kind of pattern in all this.

"Oh, *I* know she was a schemer! But did Greg? He did not. Not then. He was besotted with Tina at the time, so he had to blame the old lady. They had a frightful row . . . very publicly. He went round to the house one night, went in by the sea, shouted at her. Hazel and Henry heard, so then everyone knew. That was when Tina told him she was going to get a divorce, throw in her lot with Miss Izzy for the future. I'm afraid my brother is rather an extreme person and his temper is certainly extreme. He made threats—"

"But the police don't think—" Jemima stopped. It was clear what she meant.

Coralie swung her legs off the bar stool. Jemima handed her the huge straw bag with the Archer logo on it which she slung over her shoulder in proper Bo'lander fashion.

"How pretty," Jemima commented politely.

"I sell them at the hotel on the North Point. For a living." The remark sounded pointed. "No," Coralie went on rapidly before Jemima could say anything more on that subject, "no, of course the police don't *think*, as you put it. Greg Harrison might have assaulted Tina all right, but Greg Harrison kill Miss Izzy when he knew perfectly well that by so doing he was handing his ex-wife a fortune? No way. Not even the Bo'lander police would believe that."

Coralie Harrison sauntered off down the beach, swinging the bag which she sold "for a living." She was singing that familiar and celebrated calypso under her breath. This time Jemima Shore could swear the words ran: "This is my graveyard in the sun."

That night Jemima Shore found Joseph Archer again on the beach under the stars. But the moon had waxed since their first encounter. Now it was beginning to cast a silver pathway on the waters of the night. Nor was this meeting unplanned as that first one had been. Joseph had sent her a message that he would be free and they had agreed to meet down by the bar—and the moon and the sea.

"What do you say I'll take you on a night drive round our island, Jemima?"

"No, let's be proper Bo'landers and walk along the sands." She wanted to be alone with him, not driving past the rows of lighted tourist hotels, listening to the eternal beat of the steel bands. Jemima felt reckless enough not to

care how Joseph himself would interpret this change of
plan.

They walked for some time along the edge of the sea in
silence except for the gentle lap of the waves. After a while
Jemima took off her sandals and splashed through the warm
receding waters, and a little while after that Joseph Archer
took her hand and led her back on to the sand. The waves
grew conspicuously rougher as they rounded the point of
the first wide bay. They stood for a moment together,
Joseph and Jemima, he with his arm companionably round
her waist.

"Jemima, even without that new moon, I'm going to
wish—" Then Joseph stiffened. He dropped the encircling
arm, grabbed her shoulder and swung her round.

"Jesus, oh sweet Jesus, do you see that?"

The force of his gesture made her wince. For a moment
she was distracted by the flickering moonlit swathe on the
dark surface of the water: there were multitudinous white—
silver—horses out beyond the land where high waves were
breaking over an outcrop of rocks. She thought Joseph was
pointing out to sea. Then Jemima saw the lights.

"The Archer house!" she cried. "I thought it was shut
up." It seemed that all the lights of the house were
streaming out across the promontory on which it lay. Such
was the illumination that you might have supposed some
great ball was in progress, a thousand candles lit as in the
days of Governor Archer. More sombrely Jemima realized
that was how the plantation house must have looked on the
night of Miss Izzy's death: Tina Archer and others had born
witness to the old lady's insistence on never leaving her
house in darkness. The night her murderer had come in
from the sea: that was how the house had looked to him.

"Come on," said Joseph Archer. The moment of light-
ness—or loving perhaps? but now she would never know—

had utterly vanished. He sounded both grim and determined. "Let's go."

"To the police?"

"No, to the house. I need to know what's happening there."

As they walked rapidly, half-ran along the sands, Joseph Archer said only one thing further. "This house should have been *ours*." Ours: the people of Bow Island.

His relentlessness on the subject of the museum struck Jemima anew since her conversation with Coralie Harrison. What would a man—or a woman for that matter—do for an inheritance? And there was more than one kind of inheritance. Wasn't a national heritage as important to some people as a personal inheritance to others? Joseph Archer was above all a patriotic Bo'lander. And he had not known of the change of will on the morning after Miss Izzy's death. She herself had evidence of that. Might a man like Joseph Archer, a man who had already risen in his own world by sheer determination, decide to take the law into his own hands? In order to secure the museum for his people while there was still time?

And yet . . . Joseph Archer to kill the kind old lady who had befriended him as a boy? Batter her to death? That was what the murderer had done . . . As he strode along, so tall in the moonlight, Joseph was suddenly a complete and thus menacing enigma to Jemima.

They had reached the promontory, had scrambled up the rocks and had got as far as the first terrace when all the lights in the house went out. It was as though a switch had been thrown. Only the cold eerie glow of the moon over the sea behind them remained to illuminate the bushes, once trimmed, now wildly overgrown, and the sagging balustrades.

But Joseph did not check. He strode on, tugging at

Jemima where necessary, helping her up the flights of stone steps, some of them deeply cracked and uneven. In the darkness, Jemima could just discern that the windows of the drawing-room were still open. There had to be someone in there, someone lurking perhaps behind the ragged red brocade curtains which had once been stained by Miss Izzy's blood.

Joseph, still holding Jemima's hand, pulled her through the centre window.

There was a short cry like a suppressed scream and then a low sound as if someone was laughing at them there in the dark. An instant later, all the lights were snapped on at once.

It was Tina Archer standing before them at the door, her hand on the switch. She wore a white bandage which covered the back of her head like a turban. And she was not laughing, she was sobbing.

"Oh, it's you, Jo-seph and Miss Je-mi-ma Shore." For the first time Jemima was aware of the sing-song Bo'lander note in Tina's voice. "I was so fright-ened."

"Are you all right, Tina?" asked Jemima hastily, to cover the fact that she had been quite severely frightened herself. The atmosphere of angry tension between the two people in the room, so different in looks, yet both of them, as it happened, called Archer, was almost palpable. She felt she was in honour bound to try and relieve it. "Are you all alone?" she asked.

"The police said I could come." Tina ignored the question. "They have finished with everything here. And besides—" Her terrified sobs had vanished. There was something deliberately provocative about Tina as she moved towards them. "Why ever not?" To neither of them did she need to elaborate: the words "since it's all mine" hung in the air.

Joseph spoke for the first time since they had entered the room. "I want to look at the house," he said harshly.

"Jo-seph Archer, you get out of here. Back where you came from, back to your off-ice and that's not a great fine house." There was something almost viperish about Tina as she flung the words at him. Then she addressed Jemima placatingly, in something more like her usual sweet manner. "I'm sorry, but you see, we've not been friends since way back. And besides you gave me such a shock."

"We were once: friends." Joseph swung on his heel. "I'll see you at the funeral, Miss Tina Archer." He managed to make the words sound extraordinarily threatening. For a moment Jemima wondered: whose funeral?

That night it seemed to Jemima Shore that she hardly slept, although the fact that the threads of broken, half-remembered dreams disturbed her and made her yet more restless indicated that she must actually have fallen into some kind of doze in the hour before dawn. The light was still grey when she looked out of her shutters. The tops of the tall palms were bending: there was quite a wind.

Back on her bed, Jemima tried to recall just what she had been dreaming. There had been some pattern to it all: she knew there had. She wished rather angrily that light would suddenly break through into her sleepy mind as the sun was shortly due to break through the eastern fringe of palms on the hotel estate. No gentle, slow-developing, rosy-fingered dawn for the Caribbean: one brilliant low ray was a herald of what was to come, and then almost immediately hot relentless sunshine for the rest of the day. She needed that kind of instant clarity herself.

Hostility: that was part of it all, the nature of hostility. The hostility for example between Joseph and Tina Archer the night before, so virulent and public—with herself as the public—that it might almost have been managed for effect.

Then the management of things: Tina Archer, always managing, always a schemer as Coralie Harrison had said (and Joseph Archer too). That brought her to the other couple in this odd four-pointed drama: the Harrisons, brother and sister, or rather *half*-brother and sister: a point made by Tina to correct Miss Izzy.

More hostility: Greg who had once loved Tina and now loathed her. Joseph who had once also (perhaps) loved Tina. Coralie who had once perhaps (very much perhaps, this one) loved Joseph and certainly loathed Tina. Cute and clever little Tina Archer, the Archer Tomb, the carved figures of Sir Valentine and his wife, the inscription, "his only wife Isabella, daughter of . . ." She was beginning to float back again into sleep, as the four figures, all Bo'landers, all sharing some kind of common past, began to dance in her imagination to a calypso whose wording too was confused:

> This is your graveyard in the sun
> Where my people have toiled since time
> begun . . .

An extraordinarily loud noise on the corrugated metal roof above her head recalled her, trembling, to her senses. The racket had been quite immense: almost as if there had been an explosion or at least a missile fired at the chalet. The thought of a missile made her realize that it had in fact been a missile: it must have been a coconut which had fallen in such a startling fashion on the corrugated roof. Guests were officially warned by the hotel against sitting too close under the palm trees, whose innocuous-looking fronds could suddenly dispense their heavily lethal nuts. "COCONUTS CAN CAUSE INJURY" ran the printed notice.

"That kind of blow on my head would certainly have caused injury," thought Jemima, "if not death."

Injury, if not death. And the Archer Tomb: my only wife.

At that moment, straight on cue, the sun struck low through the bending fronds to the east and on to her shutters. And Jemima Shore realized not only why it had been done but how it had been done. Who of them all had been responsible for consigning Miss Izzy Archer to the graveyard in the sun.

The scene by the Archer Tomb a few hours later had that same strange mixture of English tradition and Bo'lander exoticism which had intrigued Jemima on her first visit to it. Only this time she had another deeper, sadder purpose than sheer tourism. Traditional English hymns were sung at the service but outside a steel band was playing: at Miss Izzy's request. She had asked for a proper Bo'lander funeral as one who had been born—and now died—on the island.

As for clothes, the Bo'landers, attending in large numbers, were by and large dressed with that extreme formality, dark suits, white shirts, ties, dark dresses, dark straw hats, even white gloves, which Jemima had observed in church-goers of a Sunday and in the Bo'lander children, all of them neatly uniformed, on their way to school. No Bow Island T-shirts were to be seen, although many of the highly coloured intricate and lavish wreaths used the familiar shape of the island's logo. The size of the crowd was undoubtedly a genuine mark of respect: whatever the disappointments of the will to their government, to the Bo'landers generally Miss Izzy Archer had been part of their heritage: the great, great, great . . . granddaughter of old Sir Valentine ("he be your Daddy and he be mine").

Tina Archer wore a black scarf wound round her head which almost totally concealed her bandage. Joseph Archer, standing far apart from her and not looking in her direction, looked both elegant and formal in his office clothes, a respectable member of the government. The Harrisons stood together, Coralie with her head mainly bowed; Greg's defiant aspect, head lifted proudly in the air, was clearly intended to give the lie to any suggestions that he had not been on the best of terms with the dead woman, whose body was even now being lowered into the family tomb.

As the coffin—so small and thus so touching in its reminder of Miss Izzy's tiny size—finally vanished from view, there was a sigh from the mourners. Miss Izzy Archer was gone. They began to sing again: a hymn, but with the steel band gently, rhythmically echoing the tune in the background.

Jemima Shore moved discreetly in the crowd and stood by the side of the tall man.

"You'll never be able to trust her," she said in a low deliberate voice. "She's managed you before, she'll manage you again. It'll be someone else who will be doing the dirty work next time. On you. You'll never be able to trust her, will you? Once a murderess, always a murderess. You may wish one day you'd finished her off."

The tall man looked down at her. Then he looked across at Tina Archer with one quick, savagely doubting look. A look towards Tina Archer Harrison, Tina his only wife.

"Why, you—" For a moment Jemima thought that Greg Harrison would actually strike her down, there at the graveside, as he had struck down old Miss Izzy, and—if only on pretence—struck down Tina herself.

"Greg, darling." It was Coralie Harrison's pathetic protesting murmur. "What are you saying to him? Explain to me," she demanded of Jemima in a voice as low as her own. But the explanations—for Coralie Harrison and the rest of Bow Island—the explanations of the conspiracy of Tina Archer and Greg Harrison were only just beginning.

The rest was up to the police who with their patient work of investigation would first amplify, then press and finally conclude the case. In the course of their investigations, the conspirators would fall apart: this time for real. To the police would fall the unpleasant duty of disentangling the new lies of Tina Archer: she would now swear that her memory had just returned, that it had been Greg who had half-killed her that night, that she had absolutely nothing to do with it . . . And Greg Harrison would denounce Tina in return, this time with genuine ferocity: "Her plan, her plan all along. She managed everything. I should never have listened to her."

Before she left Bow Island, Jemima Shore went to say goodbye to Joseph Archer, once again formally, in his Bowtown office. She did not think another tryst on the sands, night or day, would be appropriate. There were many casualties of the Archer tragedy beyond Miss Izzy herself. Poor Coralie Harrison for example, genuinely innocent, was one: she had been convinced that her brother, for all the notorious strength of his temper, would never batter down Miss Izzy to benefit his ex-wife, the woman he detested. Coralie, like the rest of Bow Island, was unaware of the whole deep plot by which Greg and Tina would publicly display their hostility, advertise their divorce and all along plan to kill Miss Izzy once the new will was signed. Greg, officially hating his ex-wife (as he had so ostentatiously made clear to Jemima that first morning by the sunny grave), would not be suspected; as for Tina, suffering such obvious injuries (carefully planned not to be *too* damaging), she could only arouse sympathy.

Another small casualty, much less important, was the romance which might, just might have developed between Joseph Archer and Jemima Shore. Now in his steamingly hot office with its perpetually moving fan, they talked of quite other things than the new moon and new wishes.

"You must be happy now: you'll get your museum," said Jemima.

"But that's not at all the way I wanted it to happen," he replied quickly. Then Joseph added, "But you know, Jemima, there has been justice done. Miss Izzy did really want us to have that National Museum, in her heart of hearts. I'd have talked her round to good sense again. If she'd lived."

"That's why he—*they*—acted when they did. They didn't dare wait, given Miss Izzy's respect for you," suggested Jemima. "One question, Joseph." She stopped, but her curiosity got the better of her. There was one thing she had to know before she left.

"Ask me whatever you like." Joseph smiled: there was a glimmer there of the handsome fisherman who had welcomed her to Bow Island, the cheerful dancing partner.

"The Archer Tomb and all that. Tina being descended from Sir Valentine's lawful second marriage. That was true?"

"Oh, that. Yes, it's true. Maybe. But it's not important to most of us here. You know something, Jemima, I too am descended from that well-known second marriage. Maybe. And a few others. Maybe. Lucie Anne had two children, don't forget, and Bo'landers have large families. It was important to Tina Archer: not to me. That's not what I want. That's all past. Miss Izzy was the last of the Archers so far as I'm concerned. Let her lie in her tomb."

"What *do* you want—for yourself? Or for Bow Island, if you prefer?"

Joseph smiled again, this time in his most friendly fashion. "Come back to Bow Island one day, Jemima. Make another programme about us, our history and all that, and I'll tell you then."

"I might just do that," said Jemima Shore, Investigator.

2
THE MOON
WAS TO BLAME

I sabel said afterwards that we were really getting too old for that sort of thing; which remains perhaps the best verdict on the whole sad affair. Unless you take the line—as my wife did—that the moon was to blame.

They've never found out who did it: just some ugly little incident among a lot of drunken campers. Since clearly none of us was involved, they let us all go and back we all came to England. Not immediately: that would have looked odd since we'd rented an expensive villa, but a little sooner than planned. You could hardly blame us for cutting short our holiday by a few days. A death on the beach below, police crawling all over the place, *Greek* police what's more: not that we put it like that to the charming young woman in the villa rental office, given that she *was* a Greek. In any case she was most understanding. Especially as we showed no signs of asking for a reduction in the rent.

Obviously none of us four was involved; how could we be involved, up on that great big villa on the rock? How could a smart villa party of well-off married people from London be involved with some little scrubber camping down below? Different worlds. Utterly different worlds. Quite soon, the police took that line too.

The world of the campers below was not only a different world, but a pretty horrible one to boot. Crowds—there must have been nearly fifty of them down there—and squalor naturally, since there was no sanitation beyond the natural shade of the olive trees, those graceful trees whose leaves had flickered so exquisitely in the sunlight on the day we arrived, when the beach was still empty.

"Do you realize that apart from anything else, apart from the noise—ye gods, the noise, we hardly slept a wink last night, did we, Isabel?—do you realize that it's *illegal*?" That was Nick. Isabel nodded vigorously; she always agreed strongly with everything that Nick said in public. (In private, since the villa walls were not entirely soundproof, we were aware that matters were somewhat different.) But my wife, Dinah, did murmur to me afterwards in that light voice of hers—the one she uses for her really snaky remarks—that it was wonderful to have Nick standing up for the law here on the tiny island of Bexi, it really must be the effect of the sun, since back on the great big island of Britain, Nick sometimes took rather a different line about the law . . .

But I had better begin at the beginning. No, not at the very beginning, not from our very first business enterprise; suffice it to say that the four of us, Dinah and myself, Nick and Isabel, had become close enough over the years to take villas together in sunny foreign parts over a considerable span of time. The Algarve, Italy, Greece (Corfu followed by Paxos), all these have produced comfortable villas, more or less, and happy holidays, of which the same could probably be said. And frankly a holiday which is more or less happy is way above most holidays you take: which is, I think, why we all persevered with the arrangement.

Did I mention that something else unites us? Beyond the same line of work and living nowadays in the same part of London. We're all childless, or effectively childless. Nick did have a son by his first marriage, I believe, but either the mother kept him to herself or Isabel dumped him—the story varies—at all events he never figures in our lives. As for ourselves, we've certainly never wanted children. We're enough for each other, always have been. I look after Dinah, she looks after me, as we're fond of saying. So that at the age when our contemporaries are spending all their time worrying over their ungrateful 20-year-olds—and a good deal of their money rescuing them from this, that and the other, also without getting much thanks—we four have the luxury of our time to ourselves. And our money, too, come to think of it.

Douceur de vivre: that's our motto (and yes, it does sound much better in French, but then we four are, I fancy, rather more enlightened in our enjoyment of luxury than the average couples who toast "the sweet life").

This year we decided to experiment with a lesser island and go to Bexi. An island paradise, said the brochure. And so I suppose it was—in a way. Much less spoilt than Corfu and much nearer to a decent airport than Paxos. Villa Aglaia was pretty near paradise too. At first. Even my wife, who generally finds something to say about the washing arrangements or lack of them, approved the separate showers for each double bedroom, to say nothing of a water supply which actually did not run out. (Remembering that time outside Portofino!) Then the view was so extraordinary, right there on the cliffs; we would look towards Albania at night, and watch the moon rise. A thin crescent the night we arrived—amusing to be drinking retsina again, once the duty-free champagne ran out—but rapidly growing.

The moon: yes. Perhaps after all Dinah was right and the moon was to blame. In so far as anyone else was to blame. Certainly the moon appears to have been to blame for what started to happen on the beach. When the first campers appeared—one large grey tent under the olives and one girl who slept under an old boat—we even thought them quite picturesque; the girl anyway. "The local Samantha Fox" my wife dubbed her on one occasion, since she certainly had the most fantastic figure, the sort you could photograph for Page Three, as we could not help noticing since she seldom wore anything but a bikini bottom.

But "Samantha Fox" wasn't quite right since Brigitte—that was actually her name—happened to be brown all over, having an amazing tan apart from having an amazing figure. As a matter of fact, I chatted to her quite a bit, in early mornings when no one else was around, and she was really very polite and friendly. Just a kid working her way around Europe as a waitress, taking a holiday on this beach in between. German probably—or was she Swedish? She had this special feeling about St. Peter's, Rome, I remember, the square at St. Peter's; she was absolutely determined to see the square. We had quite long talks about it.

Not when the others were around, however. Then, I have to say, the conversation was on a very different level. Well, we were on holiday. There was one famous occasion when Brigitte, topless, wobbled so perilously near Nick, sunbathing on the stones, on her way to the sea, that my wife and I both involuntarily looked towards Isabel.

The fact is that Isabel, who does sometimes bathe topless (but always discreetly up at the villa), does have the most lovely slim figure, everyone agrees about that. But if Isabel has a fault, it's the fact that, good-looking woman as she is,

Isabel is absolutely totally flat-chested. Perhaps that explains why I've never really fancied her, and perhaps that explains again why we've all holidayed so happily together. Be that as it may, on this occasion Isabel merely smiled in her most tranquil manner and murmured something like, "That she should be so lucky." Later, in their bedroom, however, I can tell you that it was rather a less tranquil story. What a tigress! That serene, smiling woman. Still the end of it sounded rather satisfactory; at least from Nick's point of view, and I assume Isabel's as well.

All the time, the moon was getting stronger at night; I should say bigger, but was it the increasing strength of the moonlight rather than the size of the moon itself which was so unsettling? Could you believe moonlight could be so white? Even when the moon was only half-full. That strange cold ancient light illuminating the sea which washed the rocks beneath us, the sea stretching out to the Albanian coast in a vast series of black and silver eddies with that broad flare-path in their centre. We took to sitting later and later on the terrace with our wine—a light Greek wine, for after dinner.

"So light, it's like drinking water," said Nick jovially on our second night. But of course it wasn't quite like drinking water, particularly not in the quantities in which we consumed it. Perhaps it was all that wine late at night which made us so unsettled. They were odd, quirky, even slightly sinister, those sessions we had on the terrace. (Yet hadn't we drunk wine in the Algarve? And Italy? And Paxos only the year before? The result being mere pleasure, relaxation . . .) Most unsettling of all, after we finally left the terrace, my wife and I had to lie, silent and sleepless, in our bedroom, hot behind the shutters, and listen to Isabel, the tigress of the night, who was growing more and more ferocious in the room alongside ours. Was *that* the wine?

The wine coupled with the moonlight (I noticed they did not close their shutters)? Or was it the noises coming from the beach?

For the waxing moon brought campers, more and more campers. And given its provocative light, bathing the beach in its brightness like a too well-lit stage where there had been nothing but discreet blackness before, we could hardly ignore their presence. There was—I can see it now, and my wife can see it too—a feeling of working towards some kind of climax, long before we heard the news about the party.

Besides, one or two fires began to flicker down below: those fires so dangerous to a wooden island depending on its olive groves, which was in fact the official reason for the banning of campers on Bexi. When we went down to swim in the early morning, we would find the black shells of night fires among the stones. There would also be cans of coke and beer and wine bottles abandoned. And other even more distasteful signs of what had taken place on the beach the night before. Signs of "safe sex" perhaps, but as my wife observed, wrinkling her nose (I hastily removed one of these signs from her favourite path into the water, burying it under a big cairn of pebbles), "Safe sex is all very well, but what about a beautiful beach?"

Oddly enough, Brigitte very much kept to herself apart from it all. She was friendly enough with the campers—she was a friendly girl, as I've said—but she never joined in with them at their various unpleasant goings-on. I know that, because I used to watch her sometimes from the look-out up above, watch her gazing out to sea, smoking the odd cigarette. What was she thinking about? St. Peter's square, Rome, perhaps. Something like that. But I kept all that to myself, just as I never mentioned our morning conversations before the campers came.

At least the Villa Aglaia remained airy and remote from the squalor: in the daytime, when the campers were asleep or away in the little town of Bexi, so long as you did not go down to the beach or visit the look-out, you could cut yourself off from the squalor altogether. My wife cut branches of myrtle from the bushes which lined the steep (but short) path from the villa to the beach and put them everywhere in vases in the big rooms. But as the noise grew in proportion to the number of campers, I asked my wife not to cut back any more of the myrtle: for the bushes did at least conceal the path to the villa. What if the campers, drunk—or drugged, I put nothing past them—all decided to surge up the path in the small hours?

"Then you, darling, will have to be a big he-man and protect me," said my wife in her snaky voice. "I somehow don't think Nick and Isabel would notice."

It was Nick who brought back the news of the party which was going to be held on the beach on the night of the full moon. He had been into the little port in the Landrover just before dinner—Isabel was washing her hair—to cash some travellers' cheques. He came back looking white, or as near white as anyone as perfectly cared for and turned out (which means tanned) as Nick can ever look.

"A bloody great notice!" he exploded. "In English, what's more. Full Moon Party. On Aglaia Beach—our beach. Everyone invited. Bonfires. Dancing. Naked bathing. Come by boat! Come by moped! On the night of the full moon. All this on a notice fixed to a tree just outside the town." He repeated, "And in English too."

"If it hadn't been in English, Nick," my wife pointed out reasonably enough, "you wouldn't have understood it." But Isabel, short, carefully streaked hair in a shining halo, was busy giving Nick a rewarding pat.

"Well done, Nick. At least you've warned us."

"Warned us! I damn well have. Look, I'm going to have a whisky. Have we got any left? It's a disgrace. Tomorrow I'm going to tell that little Greek girl in the office that I want it stopped, stopped without question."

"But tomorrow will be too late, Nick," my wife continued in that same reasonable voice. "Tonight is the night of the full moon. Didn't you notice last night? Very, very nearly full. Only one tiny sliver missing."

I must say that I was surprised at the time that my wife had that kind of information at her finger-tips; but then I read in one of the magazines you only read in aeroplanes that retaining the capacity to surprise your spouse is the secret of a happy marriage. I dare say that it's Dinah's remarkable sense of order which made her interested in something equally regulated like the phases of the moon.

So we come to the party. I have to admit a certain reluctance in thinking about it all, even now, back in London W11, in our beautiful house, the house which some people laughingly suggest is too big for us—"too luxurious even for you two"—but is actually a wonderful monument to my wife's exquisite, cool and above all fastidious taste. A showcase for a sense of order, somebody else said.

If that's true about our house, and it probably is, then you can just about imagine how my poor wife suffered during that nightmare build-up to the Full Moon Party on Aglaia Beach. The utter chaos, the noise of course, and the noise was indescribable, and let me not leave out the fear. The four of us, four sophisticated people, crouching there—I'm afraid after a while we were definitely crouching—as the car lights came towards the beach along the edge of the cliff, an army advancing on us, and the full moonlight lit up what went on below. In a way it reminded me of some medieval picture of Hell—all the couples writhing as though in torment, their white limbs gyrating. In fact they were of course dancing. Dancing and copulating. You would feel like using that word if you had seen what we saw.

"Supposing they decide to come up here?" Nick said that, I know he did. "Just supposing?" Nick is a big man, very heavily built in spite of all the exercise he takes. We're both of us big men, come to that, two big men with two fragile wives, that was another thing we had in common. Dinah, like Isabel, is wonderfully slender, well-preserved or whatever you call it; naturally she takes marvellous care of herself. But even Nick sounded frightened. And I was frightened too.

It was some time after that, that it happened.

"Supposing you went down there? Just supposing." Who said that? Who spoke those words? It must have been my wife for who else was present when those words were spoken? Nick and Isabel had gone off to bed at last, their shutters open to the noises of the hot, inflaming night, and the light of the coldly lustful moon. We could hear that the tigress was already devouring her huge submissive prey when those words were spoken.

The excitement comes back to me now, the secret, thrilling fear of it all, and the whispered words which went on. "Take her, you want her. She's down there. Find her and take her. You want her, don't you? Take her, you want her. Take her, you want her." Take her, you want her, wanton and naked, wanton and naked, the words became like a rhythm beating in my brain. Wanton and naked: but no, these last words were never spoken, even by my wife, but they too became like a rhythm in my brain.

Those were the words which continued to turn and tumble in my mind as I went down alone, down the myrtle path to the Aglaia Beach. It wasn't difficult to find her—Brigitte, the brown goddess of the beach. She wasn't even dancing with the others round the fire; she was sitting by the upturned boat, alone in the dark shadow cast by the boat; she was smoking one of her cigarettes and looking out to sea. Perhaps she was thinking about Rome and St. Peter's. I rather hope so. I really rather hope she was thinking about something nice. Even by the boat the noise of all the others was incredible, confusing, and they had transistors now, belting out their dance music across the moonlit sea, desecrating the moonlight, desecrating the whole Aglaia Beach.

I took her quite easily. I grabbed her, grabbed that round brown wobbly body. She was quite little really in my arms, in spite of her fullness. Much smaller than I thought she would be. So I took her and held her tight. She couldn't shout either—not that it would have mattered much if she had, the noise was so loud, the other people so busy round the bonfire—all the same I put my hand across her mouth.

"Now show me you're a man after all, a real man. Take her." But she didn't say "take" this time, but used something far rougher, cruder. That was my wife's voice again, she must have followed me down the myrtle path, but it was a voice so avid, so ferocious, that for a moment it might even have been the tigress Isabel. And besides I'd never heard my wife use a word like that in all our married life.

And I did take her. Didn't I? I would have taken her. If only she'd cooperated just a little, practised a little of that love and friendship she talked about to me on the beach. Instead she struggled: struggled rather a lot. I mean, why flaunt yourself like that, half-naked, sometimes wholly naked, if you're not prepared to cooperate just a little . . .

As to what happened after that, there's really no point in recounting it all. Sad and rather squalid really, but a complete accident. Even a misunderstanding, you could say. If it hadn't happened with me, it would have happened sooner or later with any of the other men she led on and didn't satisfy, I can tell you that.

Afterwards I hardly remembered the details of it all, isn't that odd? Just coming back so carefully and silently up the myrtle path, my wife's eyes gleaming like a cat's as we felt our way. Afterwards holding her in bed, and my wife, usually so fastidious, holding me too. Nick and Isabel were silent by then. That night, very late, it was my wife who was the tigress at the Villa Aglaia.

There's not much more to tell. As I said, the police didn't really bother us much, just a great many questions and all that, naturally; but mostly the obvious questions about the party and the noise and then the tragedy—had we heard anything, seen anything, that sort of thing, it all went on for hours.

Heard anything! Nick really snorted at that one, I can tell you. For a moment I thought he was going to start up all over again about the noise and the camping being illegal and why didn't the police stop it? Which under the circumstances wouldn't have been quite appropriate. But as a matter of fact, Nick's pretty good with the police, officials generally, knows the value of politeness and all that. He also cut quite an impressive figure, all washed and shaved and tidy.

We all were—washed and shaved and tidy. And the villa looked immaculate. As any place with my cool, collected wife at the helm invariably does.

As to Nick being so good with the police and officials generally, my wife did murmur afterwards, "Well, he's had a certain amount of practice, hasn't he?" But then as I already mentioned my wife has always been a little tart—one can't say more than that—about Nick's sharp business practices. As usual, there's a good deal to be said for her point of view.

The conversation with Nick and Isabel after the police left really rather proved her point.

First of all Isabel said, yawning slightly, "Listen, folks, we've been thinking it over; we're really getting a little old for this sort of thing, holidays à quatre, I mean. It's been great of course. No need to say that. But it's a hotel for us next year. Villas on the sea can be so noisy. You can hear everything. That's a fact. The most peculiar things. The later at night, the more peculiar. So a luxury hotel à deux, in future."

Isabel didn't seem to expect an answer to what she had just announced and I suppose there wasn't much we could say. She didn't look at either of us as she spoke. I do remember that.

Then Nick chimed in. He'd been thinking overnight as well, it seemed. And what Nick had been thinking about was the next big deal—the one where there'd been a bit of an argument seeing as I had done all the work from start to finish and couldn't see that he should have more than a very small cut. Well, on this particular deal, he simply stated that the split would be fifty-fifty. With no argument. He didn't seem to expect an answer to that one either.

As a matter of fact, I don't miss our joint holidays with Nick and Isabel. She was right, we really had grown out of all that. It's that 50 per cent which still rankles. But whenever I say so to my wife—I groan and ask: why did I agree?—she replies in her snaky voice (which generally speaking she uses a great deal less nowadays).

"You lost your head in Bexi, that's why." Then she adds more softly, "It was the moon that was to blame." There is even a voluptuous note in my wife's voice when she asks in her turn, "Wasn't it all worth it?"

3
THE BLUDE-RED WINE

The Professor suddenly held up his glass and said something which sounded like "blood-red." For a moment, in spite of the odd wording, Jemima Shore thought he was going to propose a toast although most people were still busily eating their second course. The glass was almost full. Red wine glinted in the light of the branched candlestick in the centre of the long table. A dark ruby-red: or blood-red, if the Professor preferred to put it that way.

"The blood-red wine . . . Exactly what kind of wine?" he was asking. It was not a toast. Jemima Shore felt a quick pang of relief. According to the printed programme in front of her, she was due to make her own speech—proposing the toast of the college—immediately after the Queen's health had been drunk. No toast meant no speech, or at least not yet. After-dinner speaking was not Jemima Shore's idea of fun. She did not like public speaking very much in the first place, preferring the television screen, the medium for which, as an investigative reporter and presenter, she had after all been trained. After-dinner speaking in particular gave you the whole length of the meal to dread the moment of rising to your feet, notes in hand . . .

That reminded her. Nervously Jemima checked the continued existence of those same notes in her evening bag (pretty but really much too small for this kind of thing). She had been planning her speech for weeks. It would not do to lose hold of it now.

"Chambertin nineteen seventy-six—according to what it says here." Claire Donahue had picked up the programme and was peering closely at it. She was an old friend of Jemima's from Cambridge days, hence Jemima's presence at this dinner. Claire had been a lecturer at Mallow for several years and was hoping for tenure. She had invited Jemima to speak on the dubious grounds that this would somehow advance her cause. Jemima, now regretting the weak impulse which had led her to agree—why did she always feel so sorry for Claire, for heaven's sake?—took refuge in irritation at the way Claire simply would not wear her spectacles in public. Ludicrous vanity: it could be nothing else. Surely academics were more or less *expected* to wear spectacles.

Look at Claire with that programme barely a centimetre from her pretty, pudgy little nose! Remembering the old days, Jemima decided that Claire must fancy someone or other at the dinner table. Paddy Mayall? He was a handsome hunk all right. Not quite what you expected to find at an academic dinner. The woman next but one, pale with long auburn Pre-Raphaelite hair, appeared from the seating plan to be Mrs. Mayall. Was it Jemima's imagination or was she gazing at Claire with active dislike? If Jemima's hunch was correct, no wonder. Sweet little Claire could be surprisingly predatory on occasion.

Marie Mayall . . . what did she know about her? She

had received a preliminary gossipy briefing. Ah yes, money, that was it. Her Laura Ashley dress hardly indicated an enormous income. On the other hand, a plain or plainish woman with an exceptionally handsome husband did sometimes indicate the presence of money in the contract . . . Professor Alec Redding, seated on Jemima's right, interrupted these uncharitable thoughts.

"You do realize, my dear Claire, that I am this year's President of the Wine Committee? So that I am well aware not only that this is a Chambertin but also of its precise year since I chose it myself. I hardly need reminding . . ." Pompous beast, thought Jemima, transferring her irritation to the Professor. She remembered Claire telling her that he had a reputation as a womanizer, students included, since his wife's death a few years back. That and an ostentatious taste for the good things of life, wine, even rather improbably fast cars, no, wait a minute, *vintage* cars. Long-delayed adolescence! Well, he would have to do better than that to fascinate her.

The Professor boomed on. "But then, how could you be expected to remember a little detail like the name of the President of the Wine Committee? Matters of greater import on your mind, no doubt." Greater import—what did that mean? It sounded like a swipe at Claire's private life. Perhaps she had at some point turned down the bouncy Professor. Or was it just heavy-handed academic teasing? Jemima was aware that Alec Redding was still holding up his ruby-red—or blood-red—glass. Time to catch up with Claire's *amours* later when the dreaded speech was over; Jemima was to be the guest of the college for the night. Now what was he saying?

"What *kind* of wine did the King serve? That is my precise question which I have at last happily been able to express." The Professor paused and then intoned in a suitably sonorous voice with more than a trace of a Scottish accent:

> "The King sat in Dunfermline town
> Drinking the blude-red wine . . ."

The Professor was a smallish man—if his reputation was correct, perhaps he had a short man's compensatory desire to act the lady-killer—but his head at least was impressively leonine. Now he gazed about him as though in triumph at having at last secured an audience. He proceeded to recite the next lines of the ballad, his Scottish accent becoming progressively broader:

> "O where will I get a gude sailor
> That'll sail the ships o' mine . . ."

"The tragedy of Sir Patrick Spens," commented Jemima politely. She was aware of some kind of awkwardness in the atmosphere without knowing exactly where it was focused; knowing and loving the ballad from childhood, she was happy to intervene.

> "To Noroway, to Noroway
> To Noroway o'er the foam,"

recited Jemima (but without attempting a Scots accent),

> "The King's daughter of Noroway
> Tis thou must bring her home."

"Exactly!" Professor Redding beamed at her; for a moment Jemima did glimpse his charm. There was indeed something quite boyish about him, now that he had dropped his pomposity on the subject of the Wine Committee. "Sir Patrick Spens it is. And what a tragic tale, eh? A lesson for us all. One moment there he was drinking the blude-red wine in Dunfermline town with the King and all. The next moment he had foolishly set off: to bring back his master's bride. Only to bump into a spot of bad weather on the way home. Weather rather like tonight, I fancy!"

It had been an unusually storm-tossed October; persistent rain had made it virtually impossible for Jemima to glimpse anything of the university town as she drove through. The setting of Mallow was said to resemble that of Stratford, with its medieval bridge under which flowed another rather less famous river Avon. If the weather cleared up, Jemima might inspect the charms of Mallow properly in the morning. She knew that Claire, ever-generous where her belongings were concerned, would lend her the car. In the meantime the Professor was intoning once more:

> "They hadna been a league, a league,
> A league but barely three
> When loud and boisterous grew the wind
> And gurly grew the sea."

The Professor gave due Scottish relish to the whole passage, but the word "gurly" in particular caused him to roll his tongue round it with zest. "And so they all drowned," he finished with a flourish. "That's for setting off after a glass or two of red wine."

"What is your point exactly, Alec?" The middle-aged, rather plump lady in the black crêpe evening dress had a formidable air; her spectacles at least were firmly on her nose. Jemima consulted her seating plan. Ah yes, formidable indeed. This was the celebrated Dr. Elena Kirkus: the mere sight of her name at the head of a review was enough to send aspiring young scholars' hearts into their boots. "Apart from letting us all admire your Scottish accent, an unsuspected talent, I must admit."

"Elena! Now you think I'm trespassing on your literary territory, I can see. Would I do that? *Far* too frightened; look what happened to poor Paddy here. But enough of that. What is my point, you ask. *No* point. No point at all." The Professor lowered his glass at long last. "I was merely seeking instruction. What kind of wine would they have been drinking in fourteenth-century Scotland? As a wine buff, I am always full of curiosity on these arcane matters."

"French wine, of course, imported French wine," said Paddy Mayall after a pause. "If not exactly Chambertin. I congratulate you on this, by the way, Alec. And the Pouilly-Fuissé earlier, for that matter." Paddy Mayall cleared his throat. Jemima had the impression he was speaking slightly reluctantly.

"And so a fourteenth-century Scottish king drank French wine!" Professor Redding sounded even more jovial now that he had at last got the answer to his question. He sipped at the wine in question.

Paddy Mayall looked in the direction of Dr. Kirkus. His expression was almost apprehensive. Since she said nothing, he cleared his throat again and continued. "Thirteenth-century, by the way, not fourteenth. The ballad may be based on the voyage of a Scottish princess who went to marry the King of Norway in 1281 . . . Margaret of Scotland . . . King Eric . . . a good many of her train did drown on that occasion . . ." Now Paddy Mayall began to warm to his theme. "People do sometimes think in error that it was her daughter the so-called Maid of Norway. Now she *did* die on her way back to Scotland—twelve ninety, I think you'll find—but there was no drowning involved . . . so that on the whole the evidence does suggest . . ."

To her shame Jemima's attention began to wander away during this little lecture, back to the ever-present anxiety of her speech. So that she missed the immediate preamble to the incident which followed, while witnessing the drama itself. What Jemima saw was the auburn-haired Mrs. Mayall picking up her own glass, full or full enough, of red wine, and throwing the contents across the table at the Professor. His white shirt front—like most of the men present, he was wearing a dinner jacket—suddenly revealed an enormous dark red stain; it looked as if he had been shot in some melodramatic amateur theatrical. Nor did Mrs. Mayall's accompanying words exactly undo this impression.

"That's for your bloody red wine!" she shouted, in an unmistakably genuine Scots accent. Then Marie Mayall scrambled to her feet and half-ran, half-stumbled from the high table and out of the dining hall.

Professor Redding, mopping his shirt with his hand-kerchief—which merely ruined the latter without cleaning the former—was left exclaiming in what sounded like genuine amazement, "What did I say? What did I do?"

Paddy Mayall, his handsome face flushed with embarrass-ment, got up, sat down again, and began, "Alec, I'm frightfully sorry—" Of those other diners near enough to have taken in what had occurred, Claire Donahue kept repeating "Oh God" in an apparently helpless manner, followed by, "Should I? Should I go after her, do you think?" But she sat still, Jemima noticed, and she noticed also that Paddy Mayall had fixed Claire with an uncommonly determined stare. No, Claire was not to follow.

It was left to Dr. Kirkus to say with dignity but in a voice of unmistakable reproach, "Alec, how could you? How could you be so tactless? Even cruel. And I thought you were fond of poor Marie."

Marie Mayall did not come back. A series of the diners at the high table left the hall during the rest of the meal with, Jemima suspected, the intention of persuading her to return. That might have been arguably less embarrassing than the sight of her empty place, especially since the college servants continued to plonk down portions of food there, before removing them untouched. Unlike the excellent wine, the food was rather tasteless; there was also a remarkable number of courses—or was it just the thought of the speech ahead which made Jemima feel the meal was endless? On the other hand who could tell how Marie Mayall would have behaved if she *had* chosen to return . . . Her face during her outburst had exhibited a degree of passion quite surprising in a woman at first sight shy and even withdrawn beneath her curtain of long, loose hair.

Paddy Mayall was the first to leave the hall, when his wife showed no sign of coming back. He came back a short while later without public comment. But he arched his eyebrows in the direction of Claire, who as Jemima's sponsor was seated on her left. (Mallow did not necessarily alternate the sexes in its high-table seating plan, considering that to be an old-fashioned formality.) Jemima thought that this time Paddy Mayall was silently commanding Claire to go after his wife, as previously he had adjured her silently to stay. Sure enough, Claire murmured in Jemima's ear, "Marie's awfully highly strung, as no doubt you've noticed. She's probably lurking in the Ladies in floods of tears." And she too left the hall.

Ten minutes later, Claire returned alone. Professor Redding was the next one to go, and stayed away the longest: his shirt, sopping wet and still pinkish in part, showed signs of a prolonged but clumsy repair job when he came back.

There was a little extra buzz of conversation from the students in the body of the hall at his return.

"Serve him right, the little stoat," said a student sitting at the table directly below, loud enough for Jemima at least to hear. The wine-throwing incident had certainly not passed unremarked, if its cause was not understood. For one thing, Jemima Shore's presence at the dinner—a face so familiar from television—concentrated attention upon the high table. Opinions varied, and were hotly argued on both sides, as to whether she looked older/younger/sexier/not so sexy as she did on the box. (Jemima might have been wryly amused to learn that not one single person speculated as to what she might be about to say in her speech.)

Of Jemima's immediate neighbours, Dr. Kirkus was the last to depart and the last to come back. She took the opportunity of the brief break before the speeches to stump from the hall, a heavy but dignified figure. Dr. Kirkus was the one to sort out the errant Mrs. Mayall, if anyone could: of all those present, she exuded moral authority. But her mission too was unsuccessful. She simply handed Paddy Mayall a piece of paper.

"Marie's gone home," said Dr. Kirkus. "She left this for you."

Jemima watched Paddy Mayall unfold the note and then crumple it: this time he reddened with what looked like anger. Jemima felt Claire's attention wandering away from her. They were supposed to be discussing the question of depth in television documentaries: it was already a slightly artificial conversation because Jemima was by now beginning to rehearse her speech in her mind. Since she would touch on the same subject, she was reluctant to pre-empt her arguments.

Paddy Mayall's mouth framed the words: "Marie's taken the car."

"My God," exclaimed Claire aloud, interrupting Jemima's polite response about viewers' attention-span. "I just hope she's going to be OK driving."

"Had she drunk so much?" Jemima added drily. "I rather thought the famous glass was full."

"Normally Marie doesn't drink, so she drives home. I don't know about tonight. She was in such an odd state. But it's a terrible road at the best of times, and in this weather! Dark and very twisty. Miles away from Mallow—they really shouldn't live so far out, but Marie insisted—" In her nervous state, Claire was beginning to babble.

There would be a time for all this, Jemima decided, when the great speech was safely accomplished. One way or another it could not be long now.

How would she start? "*Professors*, Ladies and Gentlemen"—sudden panic, how many professors were there actually present beyond Professor Redding? She must find out at once. Jemima began to search the seating plan earnestly for academic titles and for the time being forgot about Marie Mayall.

It was in this manner that she did not learn what it was that had so upset Paddy Mayall's wife until some time after the dinner was over. Elena Kirkus told her about it as they gathered in the Senior Common room after dinner for coffee and further drinks. Jemima by now felt the unnatural *bonhomie* of one who has been reprieved from execution—or rather, has been executed and found it did not hurt. Although her speech had been neither the best nor the worst she had ever made—after all that—it was, thank heaven, over. (And she must remember to accept no such nerve-racking invitations from old friends in future, she told herself sternly.)

"You see, poor Marie actually *comes* from Dunfermline," Dr. Kirkus was explaining. "Or more to the point, her father did. He was the man who built up all those stores from scratch. What are they called? Dunfermline Macgregor, something like that." She mentioned the name of a famous Scottish chain. "Money! Yes indeed," thought Jemima, "there must certainly be plenty of that about in Marie's family."

"You could certainly call him a king in modern terms. In any case, all that was really very close to home, the wine, the drowning and the rest of it. For a clever man, Alec can be *remarkably* imperceptive." Dr. Kirkus frowned; Jemima had a sudden vision of what it must be like to present an ill-prepared essay to Dr. Kirkus.

"The drowning—" Jemima prompted her. With her speech over, she found her curiosity about her fellow diners resurging.

"It made banner headlines at the time. A guest who drank too much and drowned on his way home. The party was at Marie's father's place on or near a river in Scotland. A bridge featured, I know that. Too much was drunk all round, whisky as well as wine, no doubt, but everyone remembered the wine because the young man who drowned had a bottle of wine with him in his car. He had taken it from the house. There was some sort of crash before the drowning, so that there was wine, red wine, everywhere when the police found him. And blood. Mixed." She paused. "I'm afraid that particular detail sunk into the public consciousness. The blude-red wine, as Alec so unfortunately phrased it."

"No wonder she was upset."

"Marie's father was much criticized at the time—and afterwards—for letting the young man go, let alone take a bottle of wine. I think the whole matter preyed on his mind. He died not long afterwards. The position he had built up—all lost as he saw it. Marie inherited everything of course." Dr. Kirkus sighed.

"Was he really so much to blame?"

"Who can tell? Difficult to control the young. We know that all right." She gestured round her, although there were in fact no students present in the Senior Common Room. "It wasn't helpful that the young man had been a kind of suitor of Marie's, I gather, and the old man didn't like him very much." Another sigh. "But Alec of all people to bring that up! He is very interested in wine, we all know that; rather boringly so, sometimes, dare I say it? But that was carrying an interest altogether too far. Alec—whom I had seen as Marie's protector in a way, since his own wife died, or at least supporter. In her not altogether happy situation. I'm sure you understand what I mean." Dr. Kirkus looked significantly towards Claire and Paddy, now having a conversation in the other corner of the room, which was all too visibly intimate. Claire looked particularly pretty, animated; she had the air of persuading Paddy to something.

"Marie and Paddy married shortly after her father's death. He was a postgraduate student up there: that's his field, Scottish studies of sorts. Too soon perhaps for either of them. It meant that Marie never went on with her own work: a pity, there's a proper intelligence there. And they really are such different characters. She's very reserved: that wine-throwing, so public, is quite a new departure. As for Paddy, I'm fond of him, but I've come to the conclusion his mind is essentially lightweight."

For all the pleasantness of her tone, Dr. Kirkus did not fail to make it clear that the word "lightweight" was, in her vocabulary, one of extreme moral disapproval. Inwardly, Jemima quailed: that kind of judgment took her back all too rapidly to Cambridge and certain dons she had known there. Had her speech been lightweight, she wondered. Could anything to do with television be other than lightweight in the opinion of Dr. Kirkus (who had, by the way, alone among the diners, not congratulated Jemima upon her performance)?

"I had to reprove Paddy just a little in a review in *Literature* once—" Elena Kirkus smiled reminiscently; her gentle smile was really more terrifying than her frown, Jemima decided. Dr. Kirkus looked round her. "Alec Redding, now, with all his faults, there's a first-rate mind. As for your young friend—"

They were interrupted by Claire herself. "Paddy's taking my car," she announced swiftly. "It's ridiculous for him to get a taxi to go all that way to that remote place at this time of night, even if he could. And of course he must go and see if Marie's all right. No, don't be silly, Paddy. How could I possibly need it myself? I'm here with Jemima till dawn, aren't I, discussing the good old days. Everyone drives my car. Everyone except Alec: he's too snobbish about cars."

"Too knowledgeable maybe: not always the same thing." It was Dr. Kirkus in her tart way who came to Alec Redding's defence, as though regretting her earlier attack. The Professor himself remained silent.

But Claire rattled on regardless, "Oh, go on, Paddy, take it."

How elated she was! And Claire's careless generosity with her possessions reminded Jemima of the vivid girl she had known at Cambridge: there was something voluptuous about such generosity, as though Claire was secretly signalling, "Have me too." Jemima was to remember that elation further on during the evening when Claire outlined in private a less than happy situation. The words, both sad and sadly familiar, tumbled out.

"She simply doesn't understand him, she can't seem to make an effort—that awful wine-throwing was about the most positive thing I remember Marie *doing* in public. She's silent most of the time. No one knows what she's thinking—" And so on and so on.

At the same time another picture was emerging, a picture of a large, comfortable country house, way beyond any don's salary, situated in a picturesque Mallow country village, far from the bustling university town. Here lived a withdrawn and wealthy woman and her good-looking unfaithful husband; and as far as Jemima could make out, there was no real sign of this ménage, happy or unhappy, coming to an end. The ugly—or encouraging—word divorce was not mentioned by Claire at any point, she noted.

At one point Claire even said, "Sometimes I hate him! I wish he were dead. No, I wish *I* were dead. It's just that I hate him for being so weak: he'll never leave her, her and her lovely money. Oh, forget it, Jemima. I think I'm rather drunk." She had indeed polished off most of a bottle of red wine, no Chambertin this, but some rougher vintage designed for late drinking when it headed in the general direction of oblivion. Jemima herself had drunk one glass and stopped.

So it could hardly have been the wine which gave her such disturbed dreams and half-waking reflections; perhaps it was the tension still lingering from her speech on the one hand and an unexpectedly fraught social evening on the other. In particular the lines of the old ballad began to weave through her brain in zany fashion, rearranging themselves in new patterns:

> The Professor held up his blude-red wine
> O who will answer this question of mine?

Other lines came back to her: the ominous presage to Sir Patrick Spens's journey when his servant had seen "the new moon with the auld one in her arms." A doomed expedition; she began to drift again and the lines drifted with her: "the new woman with the old man in her arms . . . O who will answer this question of mine?"

When Jemima did wake up to the urgent pleading summons of Claire Donahue, the latter's ravaged face and desperate cry seemed to come straight out of her threatening dream.

"He's dead," she was saying. "Oh Christ, how shall I bear it? What shall I do? He's dead—"

"Of course he's dead," muttered Jemima stupidly; she was still within the ballad's nightmare. "Sir Patrick Spens is dead." Luckily Claire did not seem to hear her.

"Paddy," she was wailing over and over again. "Paddy, oh Paddy."

Throughout the day which followed, Jemima saw it as her duty to remain in Mallow: it would hardly be honourable to depart hastily for London in the wake of such a ghastly tragedy. Besides, she could support Claire. The details of Paddy Mayall's death gradually emerged. None was pleasant. First it transpired that he had crashed his car—Claire's car—through Mallow's historic medieval bridge and into the Avon below. The car appeared to have gone out of control, or else he had taken the bridge too fast in the darkness. He had then drowned in the fast-flowing, storm-swollen river—perhaps he had hit his head first and been knocked unconscious—but that was not yet known for certain. All that was bad enough. Worse was to follow in the afternoon.

"The police," Claire said in a dull voice, tears temporarily stilled. "The police have been to see me. Because it was my car: the car he was driving, the car that crashed.

They think it may have been tampered with, fixed in some way. The brake linings were virtually severed and then—he didn't get very far, did he?" She was beginning to tremble again. "I don't understand about cars, but I wasn't careless about *that* kind of thing, it had only just come back from the garage. If someone did it on purpose, who on earth would want to kill *me*?" Claire ended on a piteous note.

Then she gasped. "Oh my God, are they suggesting *I* killed Paddy?" She began to weep again. "How could they believe that? How could anyone? He should never have been driving. If only Marie hadn't run off like that, if only Alec hadn't got going on the subject of his stupid bloody wine, oh, curse him for it—that started the whole thing off—"

"Wait a minute." The haunting images of the night were beginning to re-form in Jemima's mind, at first in spite of herself, and then in a more purposeful fashion. "O who will answer this question of mine?" She let the images have their way. She began to see what an answer to the question might be.

It was Dr. Kirkus to whom she posed it. She found the older woman seated in the college library in front of a large open book; but her attitude indicated mourning rather than reading; her spectacles lay useless beside the book.

"I was very fond of Paddy." Her manner was composed as ever. "Lightweight maybe in intelligence, but yet—" She stopped. For once Dr. Kirkus appeared to be at a loss how to go on. Jemima took the opportunity to ask her a question.

Other questions and other answers would follow. The police would later fill in all the grisly details of the truth in their patient, relentless and admirable manner. But before that process could get under way, Jemima had to put her own question.

"Why do you ask me?" Dr. Kirkus looked steadily at her.

"You have a first-class mind." Jemima's smile was not without irony. She added, "And besides, you know them."

"Yes," said Dr. Kirkus after a long silence. "It could have happened like that. It would have been in both their characters. Certainly what seemed outwardly to take place was not in either of them. So the evidence suggests—" She paused to assume her spectacles. "I was very surprised by Alec even at the time, and even more surprised by Marie." It was a judgment, the first judgment but not the last, on Professor Redding and his mistress, Marie Mayall, for the murder of her husband Paddy.

When you looked at the events of the previous night from another angle, thought Jemima afterwards, how simple they seemed: planned with the same determination as her own speech, but with none of the same reluctance. A clever man, sexually active with a taste for high living, determined to marry his less intelligent colleague's wealthy wife; the fact that the aforesaid colleague had not the sense to be faithful but actively philandered with a member of the same college was simply an added bonus. With Marie—reserved but passionate—in his thrall, it was easy for Alec Redding to devise his own very public insult: then Marie's carefully coached response followed, which got her away from the dinner and home to safety in her own car.

The inevitable offer of another car—Claire's car—came next: inevitable because Claire famously lent out her car, and since she was due to spend the night talking to her old friend she would scarcely need it herself. Redding's stained shirt was then the perfect excuse for him to leave the hall and fix the brakes . . . Redding, who was "snobbish" but also "knowledgeable" about cars . . . As for the brakes, supposing suspicion fell afterwards: where was it likely to fall but on Claire herself? Claire who was jealous of her lover's refusal to leave his rich wife.

"I wish he were dead," Claire had told Jemima in a fit of drunken despair. Might not she have told others the same story?

Even if that accident had failed, the blood—the blood red as wine—of Paddy Mayall would have flowed sooner or later. The new woman was to have the old man in her arms. Paddy Mayall's tragedy had been ordained as surely as that of Sir Patrick Spens, even if it was less noble.

4
HOUSE POISON

I can date the beginning of the whole melancholy business quite clearly. It was that bet, I said. That's what I told the detective, Tomlinson. I saw it all. I was in a privileged position, wasn't I?

"We both were," says Bella, adding in that reproving little voice of hers, "We both looked after the Colonel and Lady Sissy." Then she clicks her tongue, a thoroughly maddening habit.

To return to the beginning: the bet. Let's face it, Bella was in the kitchen and *I* was getting them their drinks, their PPs, as the Colonel always called them. PP for pre-prandial. He had nicknames for everything, everything to do with drink that is. Posties were post-prandial drinks (not many of those allowed) and MMs, mid-morning drinks, were even rarer: heavy colds or birthdays were about the only things which justified an MM in my experience.

As I told that fellow Tomlinson, the Colonel was never a heavy drinker in all the years I was at the Manor, and believe me I know what I'm talking about. But he was an *opinionated* drinker. I had to explain this several times to Tomlinson before he got the point and then he said something typical like, "He could afford to have opinions, I suppose," looking around at the Manor in that offensive way of his.

"Manor or no Manor, he was an opinionated man in every way," I countered, and, hoping to tease, "Opinionated *gentleman*, I should say." But Tomlinson just sighed, so I ended, "Naturally he had opinions about drinks."

And that was really how it all began. Drink. The papers called it "POISON AT THE MANOR HOUSE" and all that kind of rubbish, but it wasn't anything to do with the Manor, leastways not how they meant it, it was to do with whisky, whisky versus cocktails. The Colonel's "medicinal whisky" in his own phrase versus Lady Sissy's "House Poison" as she used to call her famous cocktail.

"House Poison for me, Henry," she would say in that high, fluting voice of hers. I can hear it in my ears now; odd how it carried without being half as strong as the Colonel's voice, carried right through the Manor.

"Henry!" rising on the last syllable. "Henry!" Sometimes in the kitchen Bella would put her hands over her ears.

"She's not calling *me*," she would say, as if the tone of voice was somehow my fault.

At this point I would mix Lady Sissy's special cocktail, at least on the good days I mixed it, because I'm sure I never put in half the vodka she did when she mixed it, vodka and whatever else; whereas I, I laid on the grapefruit juice pretty strong (that's what made it the *House* Poison—the grapefruit juice—as Lady Sissy explained to me when I first arrived).

"Whenever I say 'House Poison,' Henry, that's what I want."

"Why don't you just ask for poison straight up?" the

Colonel grunted. As he did, in almost exactly the same words, on so many other occasions. That was the point: the Colonel and Lady Sissy swore by their own particular tipple—no harm in that since they were rich enough to afford it, as someone like Tomlinson would be sure to point out. The trouble was that they could never leave it at that: always on at each other on the subject. All a struggle for domination, says I, having studied psychology by post a year or two back: Bella didn't approve, but I pointed out that it would help me deal with the old couple (and save me going mad with the monotony, I might have added, but didn't, Bella being obviously part of the monotony).

The only wonder was that the Colonel and Lady Sissy had been living together all these years. But then:

"No choice, have they?" says Bella; for I have to admit that it's Bella, sharp-eyes Bella, who has discovered about the contents of the will. At which point I should explain that the Colonel—Colonel the Honourable Lionel Blake, to give him his full name—and Lady Sissy—the Lady Agnes Cecilia Mary Blake, to give her hers—were brother and sister. And the will in question was their father's, the old Earl of Blakesmoor. The family estate went to the eldest son of course, and had passed in turn to *his* son, the twelfth Earl, a dreadful young man who asked us to call him Blakey. We didn't enjoy his visits, I can tell you.

"Bohemian is the word for him," says Bella on one occasion, finding him with a garlic crusher in her kitchen. (I thought I spotted an Oedipus complex there.)

To return to our couple: in his will, the old Earl had been able to separate the Manor from the family estate because it had been part of his wife's dowry. Neither the Colonel nor Lady Sissy had ever married, so the old Earl left them the Manor property jointly: on condition they lived in it together. And looked after each other. He used those very words in his will, Bella told me. If either of them left the house, the other one inherited the whole property.

So there they were, stuck with it. Although many might say that we did the looking after. But then, they were both well over 70 at the time we answered the advertisement. Did I mention that by the old Earl's will, the Manor finally got left to the survivor? Provided the Colonel and Lady Sissy had remained together, that is. Because that was the situation. And that's what lay underneath it all, in my opinion, that was the power struggle beneath the quarrelling about the drinks. Who was going to be the survivor? With the Colonel swearing that whisky made you live for ever because it was so healthy and Lady Sissy declaring in her high-pitched voice, "Live for ever, Lionel? How can you be so absurd? Whisky or no whisky, I shall outlive you, see if I don't." At which she would call for another "House Poison" and drink it with the kind of dainty relish you could see was intended to drive the Colonel mad.

All the same, for all the rows, they did manage to stick together. And they lived to a ripe old age, what's more. Which says something for both the Colonel's medicinal whisky *and* Lady Sissy's House Poison. I made Lady Sissy 80 at least when the tragedy happened and the Colonel was only a couple of years younger. Drink had certainly not cut short *their* lives. Because the Colonel was as hale and hearty an old gentleman as you could hope to find and even Lady Sissy kept on gardening right to the end. Well, they both gardened as a matter of fact, that was another thing they kept arguing about. Lady Sissy only got a bit tottery at that time of day when the cocktails had got to her, or, to put it another way, she to the cocktails. The Colonel never tottered.

If only they hadn't been quite so vigorous! So determined, both of them, to survive the other. A bit more tottering or doddering about the place and they might have been content to let nature take its course, lean on each other a bit, be glad not to be living alone like so many old people must. As it was, there was so much vigour about that the arguments if anything got worse. Especially at PP time. Which brings me to the evening of the bet.

"Lionel!" I heard her fluting away, as I stood at the drinks tray, shaking away at the silver cocktail mixer. "You've been wrong about everything for over seventy-five years! Why not admit you're wrong now?"

"Prove it, Sissy," the Colonel grunted. "Just prove it." Up till then, to be honest, I hadn't been listening very carefully; thought it was the mixture as before, as in my silver shaker.

"I *will* prove it," exclaimed Lady Sissy in a voice which was suddenly a good deal stronger, a good deal less fluttery than the voice she generally used; something of the old Earl's military bearing (there's a big portrait of him over the fireplace) had evidently got into her. Then, "Henry! Take away the Colonel's glass. No, no, you silly man. Don't fill it up."

I suppose I just stood there, staring at her. Nothing in my psychological studies had prepared me for this one, I can tell you.

And, "Give me the bottle, Henry," she went on. "We'll have it locked up. No, on second thoughts, *you* lock it up, Henry, and give me the key. There's going to be no cheating, Lionel, you've been cheating as well for over seventy-five years. The whisky will be locked up for a month. You're perfectly healthy now: we just had Dr. Salmon over and he said so. We'll have him over again at the end of the month and he'll tell us honestly whether there's any difference. I assure you, Lionel, there won't be any difference, none at all.

Then we'll know what sort of value to put on your famous medicinal whisky.

"It's a bet," she ended. "We'll write it in the betting book." This was a heavy red leather number, quite antique, with the Blakesmoor arms on it. It had once belonged to the old Earl; some of the ancient bets in it had to be read to be believed, what those officers got up to! As Bella remarked, when she was dusting it, "They didn't deserve to *have* horses, did they?"

But the Colonel and Lady Sissy had been using it for years, writing down their own bets. When I had to show it to Tomlinson, I couldn't help hoping he wouldn't go to the front of the book, the old bets being such grist to his mill, to put it mildly. But of course he did. Speechless for a while and then coming out with something predictable like, "So this is our aristocracy. Roll on the revolution."

The Colonel's bets were really quite tame stuff compared to what had gone before, Lady Sissy's too: although there were an awful lot of them. It was typical of Tomlinson that he was out to sneer at the feebleness of the old couple's bets, just after being so fearfully shocked by their father's scandalous ones.

"What a lot of fuss about—" He stopped. Well, he couldn't quite say it was a fuss about nothing, could he? In view of what had occurred. Myself, I had always looked at that red leather book as an important symbol in the power struggle, even if I was a little slow to appreciate the serious nature of this particular bet, out of all the others.

"What exactly is the bet, m'lady?" I asked politely as I carried the big book over to her. I sometimes wrote the bets down for them, and they signed them; although on this occasion it was Lady Sissy herself who wrote it down— frankly, I don't think I would have dared write it, not with the Colonel there glowering at me.

"The bet is that the Colonel will drink no whisky for a month, at the end of which he will be passed fit as a fiddle by Dr. Salmon. That's the bet. Agreed, Lionel?"

I looked at the Colonel. His face had gone quite red and for a moment I thought—but no, he recovered himself. He continued to sit there staring at Lady Sissy as if he couldn't quite believe his own ears.

"You're trying to kill me," he said at length. He spoke quite slowly as if he had just discovered something of major importance about his sister after all these years. "You're trying to kill me by robbing me of my whisky. Prove it, indeed. That'll prove nothing. Because I shall be dead, shan't I? I'll be proved right that the whisky was keeping me alive; but then it'll be too late. I'll be in my grave and you'll be alive and here at the Manor—"

"Stuff and nonsense, Lionel," replied Lady Sissy airily, as she sipped away at her own cocktail. "Since I don't believe in all this medicinal business anyway, it's my opinion that far from being in your grave you'll be in even better health at the end of the month than before! And that's what Dr. Salmon will tell us."

The Colonel continued to gaze at her.

"So what about PPs?" he asked after a while in a gruff voice. "What do I drink then? Cocoa?" By Jove, I thought, he's going to do it. He's going to take the bet. And sure enough he pulled the big red leather book towards him and signed the bet which Lady Sissy had written, with a flourish. No question about the signature there, as even Tomlinson had to agree, he entered into it of his own free will.

"You could drink some of my House—" began Lady Sissy and then thought better of it at the sight of the Colonel's beetling brows; also his face had begun to go red again.

"Some sherry, sir?" I suggested brightly.

"I shall drink nothing," pronounced the Colonel in a sonorous tone, ignoring me. "If I can't drink whisky, I shan't drink anything. I shall sit here for a month at PPs and watch you, Sissy, drink yourself to death with that disgusting mixture of yours. At the end of the month, when my constitution will have become greatly weakened and I shall therefore have won the bet, you will pay me by giving up drinking that rubbish."

"What?" Lady Sissy almost choked on her glass. "No more House Poison if you win? You're being ridiculous."

"That's the bet," said the Colonel implacably. He wrote it in the book. "Sign it, Sissy."

"What does it matter since I'm going to win?" Lady Sissy sounded quite petulant as she spoke; nevertheless she signed the book in her turn.

"You'll be grateful to me, Sissy. That rubbish is going to be the death of you one day—"

"Stuff and nonsense, Lionel," cried Lady Sissy, good humour restored as she lifted the glass which I had refilled. "Stuff and nonsense." It was her favourite expression where the Colonel was concerned. Whatever he suggested, Lady Sissy was inclined to come back at him with that phrase: "Stuff and nonsense, you're talking nonsense as usual, Lionel," she would exclaim, fluting away.

Unfortunately for once the Colonel wasn't talking stuff and nonsense. Three weeks later, it *was* the House Poison which killed her. Or rather, to be precise, it was the poison—weed-killer, paraquat—which was contained in the House Poison which killed her. Ironically enough weed-killers generally were one of the topics the Colonel and Lady Sissy were always arguing about. Always on at each other about the state of the garden shed, too, and who had the key last, that sort of thing. As I told Tomlinson, who was scarcely surprised, they used to argue about anything. And everything.

Weed-killer: a horrible death. I'm glad I wasn't present when it actually took place. The Colonel mixed that last cocktail for her himself, waiting till I was out of the room. That's what the police think must have happened. Thank God I didn't see it: it was bad enough seeing her body afterwards. Poor old girl.

But I was present when he died too, very shortly afterwards. Poor old boy. That was enough horror for me, I can tell you. He asked me for the key, looking absolutely crazy, a mad glint in his eye, his face quite red, he was breathing so heavily that I thought he was going to have a stroke. That was before I knew what he had done, of course. It seemed more natural afterwards, as I told Tomlinson, that he should be in such a state.

At the time he just asked me for the key of the whisky cupboard. "Time for my PP, Henry," was what he said, not mentioning Lady Sissy at all. It wasn't my place to question him, not my place to ask where she was, let alone my place to point out that the month wasn't quite up . . . I just gave it to him and saw him lope off in the direction of the cellar, with that curious strong stride he had, right till the very last moment a healthy vigorous man. Till he drank the whisky that is. I can still hear his cry now, ringing in my ears. I came running. Bella came running (it takes a lot to move Bella out of her kitchen but the noise of the Colonel's death throes got even Bella moving).

It was too late. You can try of course, and as I told Tomlinson we tried, all the well-known remedies, milk, bicarb., we tried everything. But it was much too late. She had absolutely laced that bottle with the stuff, knowing how he'd fall upon it once the month of the bet was over. The police told me afterwards—not Tomlinson, another man, more practical, not so full of social theories—that she'd given him a far, far bigger dose than he gave her. But then they say that, don't they? About the female of the species being deadlier than the male.

She must have planned it well in advance: they found her fingerprints all over the bottle. She must have sat there waiting for the time to be up, and knowing that the famous medicinal whisky was going to kill him. As for him, it seems that his was more of a spontaneous gesture, the weed-killer put into the cocktail shaker at the last moment, finding the sight of her drinking away at their regular PPs quite intolerable. And spiking it with the weed-killer. Mad really. Never knowing that by that time she'd done for him too. Mad really, the pair of them. Poor old boy, poor old girl; there was something childish about the pair of them, to tell you the truth, childish as well as crazy. Perhaps that's what comes of living with your brother and sister all your life. Psychologically retarded.

"Not quite natural, was it?" said Bella afterwards, clicking her tongue. "When you think of what it says in the Bible about man cleaving to his wife."

But Tomlinson put it another way. "A class tragedy" was how he saw it. In short, property had ruined their lives. Without the Manor, or the hope of the Manor, they would have been just another nice old couple living in retirement. We had to tell the police all about the quarrels, naturally, and of course the fatal bet which finally turned the Colonel's brain. Then the lawyers told the police about the will, and how everything was due to go to the survivor: that must have preyed on Lady Sissy and in the end driven her mad too.

"Property is theft," pronounced Tomlinson solemnly, with the air of one who has found the right quotation.

Property is theft indeed! I had to hide my smile. As a

detective, he really would have done far better to study psychology like me, instead of all this sociological non-sense. As I said to Bella long afterwards, when we were clearing up the Manor for the young Earl—who inherited it back again—we shan't need to go thieving in the future, now we've got enough for our own little property. A very substantial legacy indeed, on condition we stayed to the end of their lives; and nobody can say we didn't do that. It was once again sharp-eyes Bella who found out all about our legacy.

But it's no good Bella claiming credit for everything. The weed-killer was entirely my idea. Not that I handled a drop of it myself: far too dangerous. Besides, where was the need to handle the poison personally when I had all the resources of psychology at my command? The way I handled that old couple, once the fatal bet was struck, made me rather fancy myself as a kind of latter-day Iago. The gentle art was to make each of them believe the other had already done the fatal deed. So that neither of them was responsible for actually *starting* it. The poisoning, that is. Though it was never put into so many words. Certainly not by me.

You see that was quite an important notion with the Colonel and Lady Sissy. Who started the argument. Or whatever. Something childish there too, of course. How they would go on about it.

"You started it, Lionel."

"No, Sissy. This time you definitely started it."

Bella used to get quite weary with it all. But I listened all right: you never know when you can learn something helpful, where psychology is concerned. And so it proved.

I went to the Colonel, very much man to man, or rather soldier to his commanding officer. Pretty puzzled I was, about the behaviour of the memsahib. Couldn't help reporting what I'd seen, it didn't make any sense but thought he ought to know. Exactly the same approach with Lady Sissy, except of course in this case I was her humble servant, it was the bended knee stuff, if you like, rather than man to man. Same old honest bewilderment did for both, more or less the same imaginary details too. It was the timing which was tricky. Even Bella had to admire that. I brought it off to perfection.

And do you know, both of them said more or less the same thing, allowing for a few extra ripe words from the Colonel which would never have passed Lady Sissy's delicate lips.

"By God, he"—or she—"started it! I'll have you know, Henry, he"—or she—"started it."

As I was saying, Iago couldn't have done better. I tried that one on Bella but she only sniffed. It's possible of course that Bella doesn't know who Iago is, since Bella, for all her sharpness, has never really bothered to improve her mind. I sometimes wonder—

"All the same, Henry, we're a good team," said Bella suddenly, just as I was thinking about her lack of culture. Bella can be quite a mind-reader at times, even if she lacks culture. "That detective, Tomlinson, told me that it did him good to come across a proper working marriage like ours, a proper partnership. So we have to stick together, don't we? Just like the Colonel and Lady Sissy. We don't want to disappoint Tomlinson."

And Bella began sipping her pre-prandial drink—it was a sherry, as a matter of fact, a newly acquired habit with our new prosperity—with a delicate gesture that reminded me of Lady Sissy. If only Bella didn't make little sucking noises! (Lady Sissy never made any noise at all when she drank.) Ah well—

"House Poison," says I, pouring myself some of the Colonel's whisky.

5
GETTING
TO KNOW YOU

The moment the door was shut behind her, the man put the security chain across it. Then he ordered Jemima Shore to take her clothes off. All of her clothes.

"But you can leave your shoes on, if you like. They're pretty."

Jemima found that the sheer unreality of the situation prevented her from taking in what he was saying. She could hear the words all right, the man was standing right beside her, his breath on her cheek—although he was not in fact breathing particularly heavily. They were about the same height: his eyes, very widely set, the colour of glossy chestnuts, were level with hers.

The man's hair was dark, very thick and quite long; they were so close that she could see one or two silver threads in the shaggy mass. He had a moustache, sideburns, and soft dark down on his cheeks; it was that which gave him a Mediterranean look. His accent, however, faint but discernible, she could not place. He wore a clean white T-shirt with some kind of logo on it, and jeans. The broad shoulders and the heavy arms revealed by the contours of the T-shirt gave an impression of considerable physical strength, in spite of his calm breathing. Jemima was aware that he was sweating slightly.

She was carrying a large green Chanel-type handbag of quilted leather slung over her shoulder by two gilt chains. The man took the bag from her and put it carefully on the king-sized bed which dominated the hotel room. The curtains were drawn and the lamp by the bed was lit, although it was in fact only eleven o'clock in the morning.

The man repeated his command. "Take off your clothes." He added, "I want to get to know you."

It was idiotic, thought Jemima: the previous television programme she had worked on had actually been about rape. During that period, she had spoken to at least a dozen victims—of widely differing ages—on the subject. The words she had heard most frequently went something like this: "You just don't understand what it's like . . . Helplessness . . . If it's never happened to you . . . Until it's happened to you . . ."

Naturally, she had never sought to argue the point. Her intention, as an investigative television reporter, had been to present her evidence as sympathetically but candidly as possible in order to illustrate just that gulf: between sufferers and the rest, however well intentioned. The programme about rape had been the last in a series of which the overall title had been "Twice Punished": it had concentrated on the tragic social after-effects of certain crimes.

"Helplessness . . . You just don't understand . . . Until it happens to you." Now it seemed Jemima was going to find out for herself the truth of those sad, despairing cries. Rather too late for her programme. Ironically enough. And she had a feeling she was going to need all the sense of irony (or detachment) she could hang on to in the present situation. And then something more.

"Take off your clothes," repeated the man for the third time. "I want to get to know you." He was still not hurried or breathing heavily; only the slight perspiration on his upper lip betrayed any kind of agitation. Jemima now guessed him to be Moroccan or Algerian, maybe even Turkish; his actual use of English was more or less perfect.

"Who are you? And where is Clemency Vane? I have come to interview Clemency Vane." Jemima decided the best course was to ignore the ludicrous, frightening command altogether and attempt in some way to gain a mastery of the situation. She was glad to find that her own voice was absolutely steady even if she, unlike the man himself, was panting a little. She found that she was also able to manage a small, sweet, composed smile, the one the viewers loved, because Jemima generally went on to demolish the recipient of that sweet smile—some pompous political leader perhaps—politely but totally.

"Clemm-ie"—he accented the last syllable just slightly— "is not here. I have come instead. Now you will take off your clothes please. Or"—he paused as if to consider the situation in a rational manner—"I could perhaps take them off for you. But you would probably prefer to do it yourself."

The man bent forward and undid the loose drawstring tie at the neck of Jemima's cream-coloured jersey dress. His hands, like his shoulders, were large and muscular: they were covered with dark hair; the nails, Jemima noticed automatically, were very clean, as if newly scrubbed, and well-kept. He undid the first pearl button and made as if to touch the second; then he drew back.

"This is where I scream," thought Jemima. "Argument stops here. There must be somebody in earshot in this damn barn of an hotel."

"Don't touch me, please," she said aloud. "And I must tell you that, whoever you are, my camera crew are due to arrive in this room in exactly one minute; they took the next lift."

"Oh, don't be frightened." The man ignored her remark about the camera crew, which was in itself a worrying sign—since it was in fact quite untrue. Jemima doubted whether at this precise moment anyone in the world knew exactly where she was, not even Cherry, her faithful PA at Megalith Television.

"I'm not going to hurt you," he said. "Even if you scream"—he had clearly read her mind—"I shall not hurt you, only silence you with this." For the first time Jemima realized the man was carrying a large white scarf or cloth on his arm. "But please do not scream. There would be no point, I think, since both the rooms near us are empty, and the maid is far away."

The man hesitated, then he led Jemima quite gently but firmly in the direction of the large bed. They both sat down. That brought her—possibly—within reach of her green handbag; but what kind of weapon was a soft, quilted-leather handbag, however large? The man gazed at her earnestly with those wide-apart brown eyes.

"I have seen you on television, Jemima, I think you're very beautiful and you're intelligent too. I like that very much. You'll find I really appreciate your intelligence when we get to know each other better. Women should cultivate their intelligence so as to be of interest to men, how can a stupid woman be of any interest to a man . . . Education is very important for women. In order to help their man."

Now that the man was talking, almost rattling along, poking his face close to hers, talking at manic speed but not attempting otherwise to touch her or her clothing in any way, the best plan seemed to be to keep him at it.

The education of women! A bizarre subject to discuss, perhaps, under the present circumstances, but one on which Jemima did at least have strong views (if not precisely these views).

"You're absolutely right," she agreed, her tone still resolutely equable, resisting the temptation to adjust the loose tie and button of her dress.

On the subject of education, would it be a good plan or a very bad plan to reintroduce the subject of Clemency Vane? Her captor—for such he was—either knew her or knew of her. As it was, one could indeed fruitfully talk about the education of Clemency Vane, and at some length, in view of what had happened to her following that education. Had the missing Clemency been actually present in the hotel room where she promised to be, Jemima herself would have shot off some pertinent questions on the subject: even if she would have recorded the answers in her own well-trained memory (and not as yet with a camera crew). Clemency had asked for her to take no notes and certainly not use a tape recorder at these preliminary interviews. And Jemima, who at this stage was committed to nothing, Clemency having made all the running herself, had nothing to lose by agreeing to her terms.

Clemency Vane was a convicted criminal who had recently been released from prison where she had spent something over five years on a charge of drug-dealing. It was an odd case. Nobody seemed to know quite where all the money had gone: some really large sums had vanished. Jemima remembered that the original sentence had been for eight years and that Clemency had been released for good behaviour: it had certainly been a strong sentence for a first offender. On the other hand the proven details of Clemency Vane's drug-dealing were pretty strong too. And it was undeniably dealing: no question of a desperate addict merely trying to service her own expensive habit. Quite apart from the fact that she had pleaded guilty.

The oddness lay in the hint of political background to it all, a hint which mysteriously and totally disappeared when the case came to be tried and the "guilty" plea was entered. What was the country concerned? Jemima tried to remember. Red Clemmie? Blue Clemmie? *Green* Clemmie? Not the latter presumably, in view of the drug-dealing. Since none of this had finally been proffered by the defence at her trial, temporarily the name of the country eluded her: which was ridiculous. But she would have reminded herself of all the details of the case beforehand if Clemency Vane's summons to an interview in the anonymous barn of a West London hotel had not come so peremptorily to her this morning. That had altered their previous more long-term arrangement.

"No, it can't wait. I thought it could when I spoke to you originally. But now it can't."

Santangela. That was it. Santangela: one of those little states, whose precise connection with drug traffic, anti-drug traffic measures, nationalism and anti-imperialism was so difficult to establish even for those who were keenly interested. Which most Britons, and Jemima was no exception, frankly were not. That was the hint of political background which had come and then mysteriously gone away. After all, shortly after Clemency Vane had been imprisoned, there had been a successful revolution in Santangela in any case; so the whole situation had changed. Santangela: where exactly was the place? Latin America? Central America? South America? It was ridiculous to be so ignorant about sheer geography, which was after all a matter of fact. But then that was Europe-centred Britain— including Jemima Shore—for you.

Jemima looked at the man again. Not a Moroccan, an

Algerian or a Turk, then, but a Santangelino? If that was
what its nationals were called, as she seemed to remember
they were. More vagueness, she ruefully admitted. All the
same, for the first time her gaze was inquisitive, not
challenging and self-protective. A Santangelino. Somehow
connected to Clemency Vane's drug charge, once deemed
in some way political, then all of a sudden quite apolitical,
just criminal. What she was not in any way clear about as
yet was exactly how Clemency and her drugs fitted into
Jemima's current series. She had been wondering that ever
since Clemency Vane had made the first contact. But there
seemed plenty of time to find out.

Jemima's new series—very much at the planning stage—
was tentatively entitled "For the Love of the Cause." It
concerned the rival claims of public campaigning and
private life. She had already made various soundings
concerning it, had had one or two preliminary interviews
with dedicated campaigners of various sorts (including
one with a man who, very much against Jemima's own
beliefs, wanted to bring back capital punishment but whose
wife opposed him). To her irritation, she was failing to turn
up sufficient numbers of "strong women" who fitted this
particular bill; they existed all right, but preferred to keep
their private lives and/or disputes to themselves. Jemima
sympathized, of course, but remained professionally irri-
tated . . .

Then Clemency Vane telephoned out of the blue.
Jemima herself would certainly never have thought of a
reformed (one hoped) drug-dealer in connection with this
series. Yet Clemency's original call, fielded by Cherry,
indicated that this area of conflict was what she wished to
discuss. Various other calls followed, guarded conversations,
all on the telephone, with Jemima herself, with no direct
information offered absolutely pertinent to the programme,

yet a good deal of talk about the principles involved. Love and duty, their rival demands and so forth.

They had met only once: as now, in an hotel, an anonymous block in a different part of London; as now, the summons had come suddenly, giving Jemima little time to prepare.

"I can get away now," Clemency Vane had said. "Please come." And Jemima, to the sound of a few protests about workload from Cherry, had gone.

For Clemency Vane's appearance, Jemima had been dependent on the numerous newspaper and television news images from the time of her trial: the strong features, particularly the nose, which might be described kindly as patrician, otherwise beaky; the circular tinted glasses which added a somewhat owlish look; and the pretty softening halo of blonde curly hair. In fact Clemency was darker than Jemima had expected, or perhaps the blonde hair had been allowed to darken in prison; as it was her hair, also much straighter, was scraped back, and her face behind the circular tinted glasses—they at least were familiar—was virtually devoid of make-up. You got the impression of someone deliberately rendering themselves unattractive or at least unappealing; gone was the feminine softness of the prisoner on trial.

At the same time Clemency was quite tiny physically; that, along with her cultivatedly plain appearance, was another surprise. Well, you never really knew about people from their newspaper photographs, did you? That was one certain rule. Even television could be oddly delusive about size and scale.

It was still a strong face, despite the unexpectedly small scale of it all. A strong face: and a strong character too, judging from the evidence yielded up by the trial.

"I need to find out about you," Clemency had said at this

meeting. She spoke quite abruptly, dragging on her cigarette. (She had smoked throughout the interview, stubbing out each cigarette with fury when it was about half-way finished.) "I need to know if I can trust you." Her attitude was certainly not conciliatory: defiant if anything. But she was also nervous.

"As it happens, you can trust me." Jemima was prepared to be patient. "But I hope you will find that for yourself. With time. That's the best way. I'm in no hurry about this series: we've only just started to research it, as a matter of fact—'For the Love of the Cause.' It's a fascinating topic but a tricky one. I need to get exactly the right people—"

"That piece in the paper—the woman spy in love with an Israeli—"

"Ah, you saw that. I wondered. Premature, I'm afraid. She won't talk to us. Too much conflict already about what she did for love."

"I too did it for love," Clemency interrupted her. "You could say that I, too, gave up everything for love." She was busy stubbing out yet another of those wretched cigarettes and she did not look at Jemima as she spoke.

"You mean there was a man involved?" Jemima spoke tentatively. Clemency's nervousness was not perhaps surprising under the circumstances but quite marked all the same, including this sudden out-of-the-blue request for a face-to-face interview. She had no wish to frighten her off at this stage.

"Correct. There was a man." Clemency pulled on her cigarette with increasing ferocity and then once again stubbed it out.

"That didn't come out at the trial."

"I didn't want it to. I pleaded 'Guilty' and that was that."

"Is he still involved? Or rather, are you still involved with him? You were in prison a long time. Or is it over? Is it like the Love-versus-Duty question of the woman spy and the Israeli you mentioned? Is that what we might talk about on the programme?"

Jemima realized too late that she had posed too many questions too quickly. An obstinate closed expression on Clemency Vane's face warned her of her mistake.

"I don't want to say anything more at the moment. You must understand: there are problems." And Clemency declined to explain any further, sharply and inexorably. That was all Jemima was left with—until the summons this morning.

So there was a man involved. And this was him? Was Jemima now looking at the man for whom Clemency, product of a privileged education, showered with worldly advantages by her doting parents, clever enough to achieve university, achieve anything she wished in truth, had thrown it all away? Infatuation was a fascinating subject. One woman's infatuation was another woman's poison . . . Take this man. Very strong physically, perhaps (she hoped not to find out), certainly quite handsome . . . this was the man for whom a privileged English girl had wasted five years of her life. This Santangelino without even a name . . .

"My name is Alberto," he said to her with a smile— his first smile, and that might be a good sign, might it not? Once again, however, he had apparently read her thoughts—not such a good sign, that.

"First of all you will take off all these clothes. Even the shoes now. Then we will know each other better. And perhaps we will love each other." Alberto put both his big hands on her shoulders as though he were measuring her for something.

"Shouldn't we really get to know each other first?" Jemima spoke in the most reasonable tone she could muster.

She must at all costs, she knew, from studying such things, humour him: she must not arouse his violence, his hostility, give him that psychological impetus he needed to transform the situation from polite parleying to physical action. It was the feeling of helplessness that was so terrible; just as she had been told so many times.

"And perhaps we will love each other." For God's sake, it wasn't the stripping off that mattered! Jemima had a beautiful body, or at least had been assured of it enough times to lack self-consciousness on the subject. She had no particular feeling about nudity and privacy either, sunbathing topless or even naked when it seemed right without giving much thought to the subject. The exposure of her body, however disagreeable the demand in this secret claustrophobic context, was not the point. But to love each other!

How near, for example, was the hotel telephone? Looking round, she saw the telephone was on the far side of the bed. Her eye then fell on an ashtray with stubs in it. That gave her an inspiration. It was worth a try: even for a dedicated non-smoker like herself.

"Could you let me have a cigarette first, please, then I promise—"

Alberto hesitated. Finally he said, "I have no cigarettes."

Jemima gazed again at the stubs. Half-smoked. In spite of herself, she found she was trembling. And her voice shook when she spoke. She had not realized before how much she had been counting—subconsciously—on Clemency's arrival to interrupt them, somehow save her. (Clemency Vane was after all the one person in the world who really did know where she was.)

Jemima looked at the bathroom door. It was closed. She had not really thought about it but now the blank door had a sinister look. "What's happening here? Is she—wait a minute—is she *still* here? Is this a plot?"

Alberto smiled again. Jemima, her fear rising, decided that his smile was not after all a good sign.

"A plot? Yes, you could call it that," he said. "A plot to get to know you. You thought it was your plot with your silly programme about love and duty—even an intelligent woman like you, with your fine education, can be a little silly sometimes. But it was not your plot. It was our plot!"

"Clemency knows about this!" exclaimed Jemima. "Well, she must. How else did you know I was coming? Listen, Clemency's here. That's what you're saying."

"Don't you understand? Clemency would do anything for me. She's my woman. The drugs, everything, prison, that was all for me. And now she has brought you here for me. She set you up for me.

"Clemmie told me to come here," he went on with that strange, horrible exhilaration. "She laughed, yes, she laughed at you, for thinking that she would take part in your stupid programme."

He was becoming vehement again and, apparently unaware of what he was doing, tightened the grip on her arm.

"I'm a strong man, you see, the kind of man women love—women love to support and help men like me. Clemency knew that: strong man, she said, you get to know Jemima Shore then, if you want, get to know Jemima Shore if you like, because during all those years you never knew anything really about me. And now you never will. Poor Alberto, you will never know me."

Alberto's grip had loosened again, and his voice too had changed subtly as though he was imitating Clemency herself. Her abrupt, rather scornful tones. There was a silence between them.

"You will never know me." But it was Alberto who had

said that, quoting Clemency, not Jemima. It was Alberto himself imitating Clemency.

"She did do it all for me, didn't she?" He was questioning Jemima now; there was something pathetic about him, despite his fierceness, and the strong hands which still held her prisoner.

But then that temporary glimpse of something pathetic was quite gone. Alberto started to pull at Jemima's clothes. The cream jersey dress came off quite easily, or would have done so, but the very violence of his actions hindered him, those scrubbed strong hands seemingly frustrated by his own haste.

"I must not struggle," thought Jemima desperately, "I must not even scream. I know what to do, I must be passive, I must endure, I must survive. Otherwise he'll kill me." Now she was in her silk petticoat and the man was panting horribly, sweating much more. He began to talk, gabble. "Women, you like this, this is what you really want, bitches, traitors . . ." He talked on, and then half-hissed, half-shouted at her, "You I'm really going to possess—"

In spite of herself Jemima lost control. The careful passivity went. She began to struggle in Alberto's grip, to shout at him.

"Even if you killed me"—having raped me was the unspoken phrase, for, in spite of everything, she did not wish to pronounce the words—"even if you killed me, and especially if you killed me, you would not get to know me. You would not possess me."

Alberto stopped. He still held her. Now they were both sweating, panting.

"She said that, Clemency." But before Alberto spoke the words, Jemima knew the truth, understood suddenly and clearly what had been implicit all the time. What had been done for love. Once long ago. And once only recently.

"Alberto," she spoke more strongly now. "Release me. Then let me go into the bathroom."

"No. It's not right." Some of the power was waning in him, the passion. Jemima felt it. Her own increased.

"She's there. Clemmie," he added in a low voice.

"I—I want to see her," said Jemima.

"There's nothing you can do."

"You must let me go in there, there may be something I can do."

Alberto shook his head. "It's too late," he said.

"Listen, for God's sake—"

"It's too late. It was already too late when you arrived here." Now the force she had felt in him was totally extinguished. She was in command. In command as Clemency Vane had once been—had been until the very end.

"I followed her here," he went on. "I knew she was stealing out to come and see you. I pleaded with her when I got here. I knew she wanted to get out of it, I made her frightened. She told me she found me rough—but she used to like that—she called me things like demanding after she came out of prison. She said sex didn't interest her. She never, ever wanted to make love with me. She said I bored her."

Alberto began to sob convulsively.

"Then when I pressed her more, she said she never loved me in the first place. She did it all for the cause. Yet I helped her. I protected her. She wouldn't listen. The money was needed then, she said, so she did what she had to do. Now it was not. Santangela was safe. And she would tell the world why she did it all—not for me, but for the country, the cause."

He sobbed more terribly.

"For love." Clemency's words came back to her. "You

could say indeed that I gave up everything for love." Dry, wry, defiant words. But for love of the cause, not the man.

Jemima jumped up and Alberto did not even try to stop her. She pulled on her dress and he made no move to stop that either. She went into the little clean white hotel bathroom, saw the shower, the bright pristine towels on the rail, not very big towels and an unremarkable beige colour—it was that kind of hotel. All the towels were clean and untouched except one: that was the towel draped inadequately over the body lying in the bath.

The towel left the woman's face exposed, or perhaps Alberto had not wished to cover it. Certainly he had not closed Clemency Vane's eyes; they stared at Jemima, sightless and bulging, above the purple discoloration of her face, the mouth and the tongue. There was no sign of what Alberto had used to strangle her—but the memory of his strong, black-haired, well-tended, well-scrubbed-afterwards, muscular hands came back to her. The hands which had held her, Jemima. And tried to know her, as in the end they had never known Clemency Vane.

"I told you it was too late," Alberto said from the bedroom. He had not moved. "You can go away now," he added, in a remote voice, as though the subject no longer interested him. "I shan't harm you. Go. It's nothing to do with you any more."

Much later, about seven o'clock, back at the Megalith office, Cherry said to Jemima with that cheerfulness she maintained even towards the end of the office day, "Where were you this morning? There were quite a few calls. You left a message you were out seeing that woman, what's-her-name, the drug-runner who did it all for love, the persistent one who kept ringing up about the new programme. But you never left me a number. Did you see her?"

"I saw her," said Jemima. Later she would tell Cherry, of

course, as she told her everything, and later still everyone would probably know. But not just now.

"Was there anything in it for the programme?" enquired Cherry. "She was so sure she could help us."

"No, after all, nothing in it for the programme."

"Ah well," said Cherry comfortably. "You never really know about people, do you?"

Jemima Shore agreed.

6
CRY-BY-NIGHT

"I heard it again last night. That woman wailing down by the sea."

Martha James was in the act of pouring herself some more coffee from the tall black thermos. As she poured, her face under its veil of streaky fair hair was hidden from Jemima Shore.

"She sounded so unhappy. Not like a real live woman at all. I think it's a ghost." Martha's tone was purely conversational: she might have been commenting on the lights of a fishing boat seen at night, the wind which had arisen at dawn (and since dropped) or just mentioning with renewed delight the even sunshine now spreading across the terrace of the Villa Elia.

Then Jemima looked at Martha James's hands and saw that they were shaking. The coffee which she had visualized being poured confidently into the huge blue and white pottery breakfast cup was in fact being splashed into the saucer. And on to the rough blue and white tablecloth.

"Martha," exclaimed Jemima with alarm, jumping up and

taking the thermos from her. Then incredulously, "You're really upset."

Martha James stared at her for a moment. The impression given by the long straight hair and the slim figure, clearly visible since she was wearing a pink T-shirt, cherry-coloured bikini bottom and nothing else, was of youth—athletic youth at that; the legs were firm and muscled as well as brown. But Martha, when you looked into her face, was not all that young. In fact she was not really young at all. There were fine lines, a good many of them, round her eyes, despite the tan. It was the face of a middle-aged woman. This morning she also looked quite haggard. Or frightened.

Suddenly Martha smiled. She took the thermos back from Jemima, saying ruefully, "What a mess! Irini will murder me. Bad night, I'm afraid. And then that—crying I suppose it was. Kept me awake for hours. I kept thinking I should do something. Thus: the shaking hand of Martha James, the ruined tablecloth of our dear Irini. A cup of coffee is definitely the answer. If I can somehow get it into the cup."

"Have a fresh cup." There were still a few unused ones on the long wooden table which served for all their meals on the terrace.

"A fresh cup and a fresh start. Most appropriate to this holiday." Martha sat down and began drinking composedly. The moment of anguish, fear or whatever it was had evidently passed. Jemima Shore decided to forget the incident: this despite her own slightly unruly curiosity—the quality after all which had made her into a leading television investigative reporter. She had, as she then believed, other more urgent matters to preoccupy her.

Jemima Shore thought instead about the subject of fresh starts. It was, as Martha had observed, appropriate to the holiday and, for that matter, appropriate to Jemima's own presence on the island of Corfu.

The party now staying at the Villa Elia, situated just above a small beach beside a rocky headland, was not exactly a party in the strict sense of the word. That is to say, according to the hostess, Alice Garland, none of the guests had been known to her in advance. They were also all paying—quite heavily—for the privilege of being there in the first place. That included Jemima Shore herself (although Megalith Television, her employer, would end by picking up the tab). The important point was that she was receiving no reduction from the full rate, despite the handsome offers made by her hostess.

"But you really needn't pay! Not the whole amount, at least. After all, if you *did* make a programme about our little party venture, it would be the making of us!" Alice Garland had sounded appealingly wistful in London. But then she nearly always did sound wistful, Jemima decided. Even in her London clothes—check jacket, white silk blouse, short black skirt—Alice had the air of an elegantly dressed doll. She certainly looked too young and virginal to be running her own business, despite having a husband—somewhere— no further details given. At the Villa Elia itself, straight hair falling, she looked a positive infant. It was in fact the same kind of pretty light-and-dark hair as Martha's and the two women were not so dissimilar in type. But Alice's face was genuinely youthful; standing beside her, Martha looked a rather weary echo.

Long before she reached Corfu, Jemima Shore had however appreciated that there was nothing notably childish about Alice Garland's business methods. Alice was—justifiably of course—quite determined to make her so-called "Fresh Perspective Holidays" a success; but Jemima fancied that Alice could probably show herself quite ruthless if the occasion offered, beneath that naïve exterior. Alice, yes. But this Alice was hardly in Wonderland. She was in business in London and Corfu, competing with a number of tour operators, not by offering cut prices—far from it—but by offering a holiday of a particular, and rather special, type.

Fresh Perspectives, as advertised, were for those who felt themselves to be at some kind of turning-point in their lives; it might be marital, professional, spiritual or all three. Whatever its nature—with which Fresh Perspectives was not concerned—"guests" took advantage of some weeks at the Villa Elia to contemplate this turning-point. There was only one theoretical condition laid down: guests were supposed to arrive solo, spouses, live-in-lovers, companions, mere friends being none of them officially welcome.

"And if a fresh perspective on life happens to include encountering a fresh partner at the Villa Elia?" Jemima had asked Alice.

"Naturally it happens," Alice had replied in her soft little-girl voice. "At least I presume it happens, human nature being what it is. We wouldn't know of course. Most people don't sleep in the house, only the officially elderly or infirm. People who might have some difficulty making their way to the various guest-houses scattered about the property at night. And we don't get many of those, as you will see. But in any case one of the things which prevents the burgeoning of 'Fresh Perspective' romances, even in this day and age, is the fact that far more women than men seem to want to come." Alice smiled enchantingly. "I suppose it means that far more women than men need to make a fresh start in life," she added.

"It may mean that," commented Jemima drily. "Or it may simply mean that more women than men have the courage to realize it." Was there perhaps something smug about this elfin creature, with her husband and her rapidly expanding business? You could not imagine Alice Garland herself needing to make a fresh start . . . but if she did, plenty of people would want to help her do it. For Alice was one of those people who had the effect, consciously or unconsciously, Jemima had yet to decide, of arousing a kind of hero-worship in those around her; or just a desire, quite simply, to be in her presence. Jemima had once or twice surprised Martha James, for example, gazing at Alice with a kind of yearning. Another of the guests, a somewhat older woman called Mrs. Vascoe, was inclined to try and engage Alice in earnest private conversation whenever possible. (Then Jemima reflected that Mrs. Vascoe, although dressed in a much older style, was probably not much older than Martha James in years.)

Looking at Martha James now, Jemima wondered precisely what kind of turning-point it was that she had reached. Martha was a painter: Jemima recognized the name although she had not heard of her work for some years. Was that the problem? Waning fame? Waning inspiration? Some other kind of distraction? At the Villa Elia it was in any case a camera not a sketch-book which was generally to be found in her hand. And Jemima had happened upon Martha once or twice taking photographs in the maze of paths bordered with rosemary and other odorous shrubs which led among the various cottages. You stopped on a path, turned, and there was the cerulean sea below you, framed by rocks. The views sprang up, fell away, emerged, vanished, in seemingly artless fashion; until you gradually realized that the vistas of the Villa Elia, like everything else to do with it, must have been carefully planned.

If Martha James was not to be found painting or sketching, another of the guests had recently started to parade a sketch-book. This was an American girl in, say, her early 30s, called Felicity Dalbo but known at her own request by the nickname of "Fizzy." As Martha might be surprised with her camera, Fizzy could be seen, rather more ostentatiously, placed in the centre of a popular path, with her sketch-book. Fizzy was actually Alice Garland's greatest fan: if Martha followed Alice about—sometimes—with her eyes and Mrs. Vascoe requested little chats with her, Fizzy was publicly loud in her admiration for everything Alice did or said.

"This villa! Isn't it something?" she exclaimed several times a day. "How I wish I could get it all together like Alice—maybe I *will* when I've been here long enough!"

The results of Fizzy's artistic labours had a slightly primitive air. The bright blue shutters of the villa, actually folded flat against the white-washed walls, sprang out at you in Fizzy's water-colour as though with an energy of their own; they were also way out of scale. All the same, Jemima found Fizzy's various efforts not unpleasing: like Fizzy herself, they conveyed a certain indomitable cheerfulness. Jemima was a good deal more doubtful about Fizzy's habit of producing her latest sketch—and she worked rapidly—at lunchtime.

"Go on. Criticize it. You can say whatever you like. I want to learn, dammit," Fizzy would say, smiling eagerly at one of the other guests. Fizzy, it was clear, was not a professional painter, nor was her turning-point to be supposed to concern "art." In any case, Fizzy herself had left no doubts on that score.

"Bad marriage," she had announced at large to the company at the pre-dinner drink session on the day of her arrival. They were drinking a delicious local white wine called Boutari (with the exception of Martha who always drank water). "Or rather a good marriage to a bad guy. 'Fizzy

Dalbo,' I said to myself one day, 'you just don't have to live with this man any more. The compromises you have been making are just not acceptable for a woman in the eighties. It's yourself you have to live with. That's the bottom line. Learn how to do it, why don't you?' So here I am." Fizzy gave a wide smile, displaying her large and even white teeth. It was the beauty of the teeth, thought Jemima, more than anything else, which revealed Fizzy's transatlantic origins; Fizzy herself had been and possibly still was working for some English publisher in London. And Fizzy's unsatisfactory husband had, it seemed, been English.

"Not a reticent character," had been Martha James's comment to Jemima, after Fizzy, large tote bag over her shoulder, a fresh glass of Boutari in her hand, had swept off to unpack.

"It's so wonderfully tranquil here, isn't it?" murmured one of the other guests rather nervously after a short silence. Sarah Halliwell was a gentle girl, dressed in a green and gold shirt of Indian design, with thick, shining hair coiled at the moment but which loose could reach to her waist. She obviously had some Indian blood: the mixture of Indian and European had produced in her a lovely delicate bone structure which put even Alice Garland's physical neatness to shame. But for all her elegance Sarah had a haunted air. To Jemima, she spoke briefly of "a betrayal where I had least expected it. Perhaps with hindsight I should have done so." She said nothing about what that "betrayal" might have been. "A fresh perspective was certainly necessary in my case," she ended.

Jemima forbore to ask any questions. She was after all looking for ideas not material. Were she to decide to include some film of the villa in her planned series (tentatively entitled "Possible Dream? Starting All Over Again") it would obviously not be this party she dealt with.

For one thing, all guests interviewed on television would have to give their permission in advance. But she did note that Sarah spent a lot of her time reading abstruse-looking journals with titles like *Classical History* and *Graeco-Roman World*. She also, alone of the party, spoke some modern Greek. For Sarah Halliwell at least, the choice of a Greek island like Corfu for her repose did not seem to be a coincidence. As for Sarah's comment concerning Fizzy, it was clear to Jemima that what she really meant was: "Is Fizzy going to ruin all our precious tranquillity?"

So far Martha had not been asked to give an opinion of Fizzy's work, despite her professional qualifications to do so. Perhaps it was unfortunate, thought Jemima, that Fizzy chose the lunchtime following Martha's nerve-wracked coffee drinking to do so. The session was as usual held on the terrace, Fizzy with the first Boutari of the day ("I guess I deserve this") in her hand. The conversation certainly got off to an uncomfortable start. Besides which, there was undoubtedly an element of rivalry or jealousy between Martha and Fizzy over the subject of Alice, all the stronger because it was generally unspoken.

"Fizzy, that's my cottage you've been painting," exclaimed Martha abruptly. "Well, I think that's quite a—" She stopped. The missing word was not going to be a pleasant one. Cheek? Yet once again Martha looked frightened, or at any rate more upset than angry.

"Why, Martha, don't be piggy," and Fizzy gave a good-humoured pat to Martha's thin brown arm; she touched people a lot, Jemima noticed. Martha moved away immediately; unlike Fizzy, Martha went out of her way to avoid physical contact.

"Gee, I'm sorry. But you know me, I guess I go everywhere just looking at it all, just loving it all. Nothing personal. I certainly did not mean to invade your space. I really respect your need for privacy. Hey, I'm like that myself. We're all like that here. It's just that your cottage being on its own. Furthest away from the house and being on that kind of real cliff over the beach. And the cute headland on the other side of the bay. You were out—"

"How did you know I was out?" But before Fizzy could answer with another long explanation—she really did talk a lot especially when embarrassed—Martha seized Fizzy's sketch-book and made a rapid and not unkindly assessment. She finished, "For an amateur and I take it a beginner, it's not at all bad." Martha even managed a rather strained smile. "I wish I had your freshness, Fizzy."

"Fresh Fizzy, fresh perspective—fresh! That's me all over. Thank you, Martha. Thank you very much. And to show you I mean it I promise I'll never come and paint near your cottage again, in spite of the glorious view, not even if you beg me. I won't come near it, not even if you start calling out for help in your lonely cottage in the middle of the night."

But Martha merely lit a cigarette—she was the only guest who smoked and made up for it by smoking quite a lot—and moved away. After a while she sat down in the basket chair slightly apart from the others, which commanded the best view, at least from the terrace. The branches of an olive tree, one of the many from which the villa took its name, framed the exit to the pathway which wound down to the beach; the blue, blue sea lay beyond. Pots of plumbago with its bright green leaves and profuse pale blue flowers flanked the exit. Everything at the villa, from cushions to flowers, had some kind of blue theme; chosen perhaps for repose or perhaps to remind you of the ever-present sea below and stretching out to the horizon.

"My favourite colour—blue," Alice Garland had announced on Jemima's arrival.

"A cold colour, too many blues make a house heartless," Jemima's chic decorator friend Daisy had once said: but of course that warning judgment could not be true in Greece, on the edge of the sea.

"Talking of crying out in the night," said the fourth guest, Mrs. Vascoe, conversationally, "did anyone else hear that owl or cat or dog or whatever it was howling again last night? Down by the beach." Betsy Vascoe, being the sort of apologetic person who always chose the least comfortable chair in the worst position, Jemima noted, spoke from a basket chair which was rammed up against the lunch table. In her staid summer clothes—she was the only one of them who habitually wore blouses and skirts in the daytime—she had altogether an old-fashioned air. When she said things like "all you young things" nobody, not even Martha, sought to contradict her. "Alice running this place with all her wonderful youthful efficiency"—That was Betsy Vascoe's frequently heard paean of admiration.

Now there was a crash of glass as something fell heavily on the marble-flagged terrace. Jemima looked sharply in the direction of Martha. But Martha, still with her back to the company, smoking and looking out to sea, had not moved.

"I'm so sorry!" exclaimed Mrs. Vascoe, jumping up as if personally responsible for the accident and beginning to dab away at the pool of white wine on the floor with her white shirt-tails. But it was Sarah Halliwell's glass which had crashed, not hers. At the noise of the crash, Irini, the Greek cook, came springing out of the kitchen and, moving lightly despite her formidable bulk, quickly and expertly cleared it up.

Alice Garland appeared at the same moment. She had the air of being about to go shooting: she had a basket over her arm and wore a big Greek straw hat which shadowed her face.

"Hey, Alice," cried Fizzy, "is there some kind of ghost here which hoots or howls? Betsy heard it last night. Some of us heard it the other night. Bright idea coming up, maybe it's the ghost of our various *pasts* trying to stop us making a fresh start. Howling at us." Fizzy shivered in an exaggerated manner and looked around, as if for applause.

"Anyone else hear this howling last night?" asked Alice pleasantly. "Jemima? Fizzy? Sarah?"

Sarah shook her head. "Not last night." Nobody else said anything.

"Martha?"

"I heard nothing last night," replied Martha James without looking round.

"So it seems you were the only one disturbed, Betsy," concluded Alice. "But then, your cottage is closest to the sea. As a matter of fact it's a bird, you know. A local bird. But to the imaginative"—she smiled in Mrs. Vascoe's direction—"I suppose it could sound like a woman, an unhappy woman at that."

"Oh, Alice, I wasn't complaining," said Mrs. Vascoe hastily, "I'm probably quite wrong about the whole thing."

A fresh start for Betsy Vascoe should certainly include learning how to stand up for herself, thought Jemima. She understood that Mrs. Vascoe was recently widowed; Jemima guessed her late husband to have been a man of strong character. Betsy Vascoe, otherwise, spent a lot of time studying guide books to Corfu and was the only member of the party who actually ventured to the museum in the town.

Then Jemima forgot Mrs. Vascoe as she concentrated on wondering why Martha James—so preoccupied with the "wailing" at breakfast—had suddenly denied it at lunch. Besides, Alice Garland was wrong: the closest cottage to the sea was not Mrs. Vascoe's, it was Martha's.

Before Alice could say anything more, reassuring or otherwise, to Betsy, Irini, now laying the table for their usual cold lunch of stuffed vine leaves, taramasalata and salad, said something raucous in Greek.

Alice frowned.

"What did she say?" asked Fizzy, and when Alice still frowned, "Sarah?"

Sarah Halliwell glanced carefully at Irini, who laughed back at her. "She says we are too many women here. We are needing a man. So someone here is calling out for a man in the middle of the night." Irini nodded vigorously and added something else. "She says *she* needs a man too." Irini roared with laughter. So far as could be ascertained, Irini like Mrs. Vascoe was a widow: there was no sign of a husband, and a son, Nikos, helped her with the work of the villa which could not be done by the maid Maria: he also operated the boat. Actually Nikos, despite his youth, was altogether a much less imposing figure than the substantial Irini with her fine strong features and mass of greying black hair.

"You need a man, Irini my love, you got a man." The voice—male—was so unexpected, coming as it were out of one of the rosemary bushes on the path, that it seemed to Jemima that all the women on the terrace jumped. Afterwards she would come to revise that opinion: all the women had jumped except one.

A minute later the head of a man appeared coming up the path from the sea, and a minute after that the man himself. He was tall, almost burly, dressed incongruously in dark grey trousers and a dark grey jacket. His white shirt was, however, open at the neck; there were signs of a tie hanging out of his pocket, its end trailing. His hair was golden brown, very curly, rather long; his complexion was ruddy rather than brown, however, or perhaps that was the effect of sun on his particular kind of rather florid good looks. For he *was* good-looking, even if at the same time he gave the impression of having gone to seed.

The man before them was not carrying a suitcase or indeed any kind of bag, but his shoes, leather brogues rather scuffed, were in his hand. He had evidently come off a boat on to the beach below. It was perfectly possible to arrive at the villa like this: in fact it was easier than using the precipitous narrow path down from the village winding its way through olive groves, the journey taking about thirty minutes altogether. Luggage and other supplies were as a result generally brought in by Nikos's boat from the next-door bay.

"I suppose Nikos is really the power behind the throne in this place," Sarah Halliwell had observed thoughtfully on the subject of the handsome silent Greek youth. "Being in charge of the boat and all that; he's the only one who can come and go as he likes, night and day."

"Then Irini is actually *on* the throne!" answered Alice with a light laugh.

"Oh, no, Alice, you're on the throne." That was Fizzy. Really, thought Jemima, she went too far sometimes.

Elia Beach itself was not of course private—all beaches in Greece being public by law. But since access to it was in effect only by boat (you would have to know the area well to discover the entrance to the village path) tourists only congregated there in the middle of the day. Very occasionally an intrepid couple slept over amid the pebbles and were noticed by Jemima if she had a pre-breakfast swim.

At the moment the happy cries of the said tourists could be heard as a background to the strange scene of arrival on the terrace. How different were sounds heard in the bright, shadowless sunlight of the day! Could the cry-by-night have been merely an ecstatic nocturnal tourist? There were some ecstatic ones, and some loud-mouthed ones too (a horde of Italians doing gym on the shore at midday two days previously came to mind). There were some ecstatic sunbathers too: topless ones, some brown and shapely, pagan nymphs fitting into the Greek landscape; some it had to be said (like Fizzy, who alone of the party sometimes went topless) neither brown nor shapely, who should not have risked the exposure . . .

"Kirie William! So you do come,"cried Irini with much enthusiasm, launching herself on the stranger and embracing him with fervour.

At roughly the same time Alice said, "William!" in a voice which contained not even the pretence of welcome. "What are you doing here?"

"Like the rest of you, my dear Alice, making a fresh start. And with quite as much reason, I think you'll agree." He bowed. "William Gearhart—at all your services."

"William"—Alice paused—"William is my husband."

In contrast to her chilly tone, William Gearhart's was positively ebullient. "Do I get some lunch, Irini? No, wait a minute, what I really want is a drink. Don't worry, I can pay my whack, or rather my whackette. What's she charging you these days?" he enquired at large, as he pulled at his pocket, producing the rest of the tie and a lot of soggy-looking drachmas in rather small denominations. As Irini hastily brought forward bottle and glass, Jemima realized that what William Gearhart's flushed look really signified was not the beginning of a tan but the end of a drinking bout. Drinks at the airport? In the aeroplane? In the town? In the village? It was not difficult to get a drink in hospitable Corfu.

It was tempting to regard the arrival of William Gearhart at the Fresh Perspectives "house party" as being annoyingly disruptive: people united in a desire for a quiet life found themselves unwillingly plunged into a more lively situation.

But had there not been strains all along, beneath the surface of the party, Jemima wondered. The mysterious cry-by-night—as Fizzy would have it, "our pasts calling out to us"—did that carry with it a warning?

As she reflected, William was busy greeting Martha James with a special flourish. "Martha James! The famous painter I do believe!" Martha nodded in William's direction. "The once and future famous painter! A fresh start for Martha James! No more naughty—whoops!" William Gearhart clapped a hand over his mouth.

"William!" Alice's rigid self-control sounded as if it might be slipping.

"It's all right, it's all right, I've said nothing, now have I? Are you painting anything hereabouts, Martha? I should be most interested to see your latest work. Or are there any *old* paintings to be seen?" He gave Martha a look which was almost a leer.

It was with the helpful air of one smoothing over a difficult situation that Fizzy said rather breathlessly, "I guess I'm the only working artist around here, and I'd just love to get some fresh perspective on that—"

"Good afternoon, Mr. Gearhart, we've met before, as you may remember. Sarah Halliwell from the Graeco-Roman Institute." Except that she had virtually interrupted Fizzy, Sarah sounded not only gentle as ever but absolutely composed.

"The beautiful and brilliant Miss Halliwell! How could I forget you, or anything about you? Now why I wonder are you here? But I mustn't be a tease. She won't like it. My dear wife. My good wife Alice. Alice Garland as we must call her." He sat down rather heavily and gazed with some surprise at the glass before him, now empty.

"Can I stay?" he asked, rather pleadingly. "I have to talk to you, Alice. About *business* matters. You know what I mean." He counted the guests. "There must be an empty cottage if you don't want me in the house."

"You can stay." But Jemima got the distinct impression that Alice was agreeing more to stop her husband talking further than for any more hospitable reason. Her pretty face had certainly formed into a formidable frown at the mention of the word "business."

"Thanks," William said. "Actually I don't want any lunch. And I don't want any dinner either. Just sleep. And later maybe a swim. I'll see you all tomorrow morning. And I'll be very, very good."

After William Gearhart had lumbered away—to the cottage next to Jemima's—Alice took a deep breath and faced them. The smile she wore had the air of being etched upon her features.

"How can I explain? And you were supposed to be having peace. William was, is my husband, that is we're separated not divorced. I took the name Garland instead of Gearhart—for business purposes. Yes, William does need a fresh perspective. You see he once owned a gallery for selling antiquities. There was some trouble. I won't go into it. Some of them weren't quite what they seemed to be. Fakes in short. Some of them turned out to have reached England, unlawfully, by a rather odd route. I won't go into that either. There was a case. William was acquitted. But of course his reputation! And at the same time our marriage broke up. It didn't—how can I put it? It didn't survive the strain of something like that. The gallery had to close. He's had a hard time." She paused. "And so in a way have I. I've tried very hard to build up Fresh Perspectives in some ways as a kind of therapy—but I'm not asking for your pity."

Unexpectedly Mrs. Vascoe was the first to speak after Alice finished.

"Thank you for being so frank, my dear. You know how

much we all admire what you're doing here. And I'm sure we can all sympathize with someone who has gone through a hard time. In our different ways, so have we."

"How true," murmured Sarah. She touched her brow with her handkerchief. "It is hot, isn't it? I don't think I want any lunch after all. I'll go back to my cottage and lie down for a while."

As she departed, Fizzy gazed after the gracefully swaying figure vanishing among the rosemary bushes. "So she knew him." Fizzy sounded puzzled, ruminative, as though working something out. Only Martha said nothing at all about Alice Garland's form of personal statement. But the haggard look, the look of fear so striking on her face at breakfast time, had returned.

In bed in her cottage, Jemima could not easily get to sleep. A light breeze generally sprang up with the darkness to alleviate the close heat of the day, and there was always the ceaseless noise of the cicadas to soothe her. Tonight the cicadas sounded almost too loud for sleep; dropping off for a brief moment, she decided they were trying to tell her something, but awake once more, she knew that to be mere fancy. All the same, even her favourite lullaby of the sea pounding the shore below was more disturbing than restful tonight.

Somewhere—one of the other cottages or was it up at the house?—a shutter banged heavily. They were all supposed to fasten their shutters at night to prevent this very thing happening. Someone had forgotten. More banging, was that what was disturbing her? Jemima decided to ignore it and pulled the pillow firmly over her head.

Dinner had been a subdued affair for all Irini's delicious lamb roasted in the Greek manner—no William Gearhart and no Sarah either for that matter; the latter, like William, had remained secluded since the pre-lunch scene on the terrace. Jemima thought again about William Gearhart's arrival and Fizzy's remark, gazing after Sarah's retreating back: "So she knew him." She thought about Martha James: "I heard the woman wailing." A local bird? A bird called cry-by-night? She began to drift once more towards sleep.

Either the banging shutter or some other noise woke Jemima; this time she knew from her clock that she had been asleep for some time. Feeling that she had awoken at the end of the noise, whatever it was, Jemima jumped up and looked out of her bedroom window in the direction of the sea. Her view of the shore, either from her bedroom or from her small sitting-room, was obscured by some of the olive trees.

Was that someone down there on the shore or merely the shadow of a rock? It was impossible to be certain at this distance. The beach was predominantly pebbled, but the headlands on either side had left a deposit of fallen rocks and stones, some of them quite large. A flickering light or the flashing of fishing lights out to sea? (Irini told them that Nikos regularly went night fishing, like the other men living round about.) Was that a boat? But from inside her cottage Jemima could not see the little stone pier running into the sea where Nikos usually kept his boat fastened.

Rather gingerly, she stepped out on to her little terrace. Someone wailing below, a cat, a dog, a bird—or sheer imagination in the shadowy, post-midnight world, the so-called dead hour of the night?

The soft, warm darkness was quite opaque. The stars over their heads at dinner had been brilliant and numerous in the lofty black bowl of the sky. Mrs. Vascoe—her shyness was rapidly evaporating—had given them a lesson in how to name them: "Follow the line of the Plough, it's quite easy after that." Now the stars were all gone. The promising half-moon which Jemima had observed behind racing clouds was also no longer to be seen. Only the cicadas kept up their ceaseless chatter, and far below the sea rushed relentlessly to and fro on the beach.

Up at the house, Jemima was surprised to notice that the terrace light—generally left burning—had been switched off. Equally surprising, the lights of Fizzy's cottage were burning, not just the bedroom light but the light of the small sitting-room as well.

And the banging, yes, the banging was coming from the direction of Fizzy's cottage.

After a moment, surprise gave way to a reluctant but undeniable feeling of alarm. Jemima took a look round towards the other cottages, William Gearhart's was quite dark; she expected that; she had seen no lights there at any point during the evening, either when it began to get dark before dinner or later on her return. A fresh start meant sleeping it off: yes indeed! As far as Jemima was aware, Gearhart had been comatose since he lumbered away before lunch.

The small light over Sarah Halliwell's terrace was still burning but the rest of the cottage was plunged in darkness; that too was to be expected; Sarah always slept with the terrace light burning, unlike Jemima who feared for the insect life the light might attract.

"There are other things to fear beyond insects," Sarah had murmured. "As a matter of fact, I don't like the dark very much, if you want to know. Childish, I dare say."

Jemima could only glimpse the roof of Mrs. Vascoe's cottage, or where she imagined it to be; no pool of light there, however. Martha James's cottage in its isolated position could not be seen at all.

Fizzy's words came back to her: "If you cry out for help in the middle of the night . . ." It was an uncomfortable realization under the circumstances that Martha's cries for help would not indeed be heard. By the rest of the guests, that is, if they were safely installed in their own cottages. Why was she thinking about Martha? It was Fizzy's cottage which should be occupying her thoughts.

Was she to investigate? The correct answer was: yes. Otherwise the restlessness might continue till dawn, with the addition of a faint, nagging guilt, not that she seriously thought anything was wrong, all the same . . . Yes, she would investigate. Once the decision had been reached, the taking along of a torch seemed a good practical plan, unfanciful and thus reassuring. She hardly wanted to cause her own incident by falling off one of the steep paths into the shrubby bushes, let alone down a cliff. Jemima located her torch, remembered that the battery was low and that she had forgotten to do anything about it, put on her flip-flops, pulled her cotton robe closely round her and set off.

Halfway down the path to Fizzy's cottage, the torch petered out. Jemima sighed. On the one hand she could return (but she had still not switched on her own terrace light because of the insects). On the other hand the lights of Fizzy's cottage beckoned—even if she would not quite have put it like that. She decided to go on.

There was no more wailing from the beach, no other sound but the occasional bang of the vagabond shutter ahead and the persistent susurration of the cicadas. Her strongest sensation at this point was in fact of smell: the rich scent of rosemary, oregano and sage as she brushed through the Mediterranean night.

Jemima reached Fizzy's cottage and peered through the open French windows. The little sitting-room with its simple blue and white furnishings was demonstrably empty. No one could have hidden behind that white cane chair or sofa, let alone beneath the spartan white cane tables, two or three of them, all smothered in Fizzy's books.

Should she go further? The shutter banged again; she realized that the sound was at the back and that it must be a bedroom shutter. That decided her. Jemima, useless torch still in hand, advanced. The bedroom, like a sitting-room (and like Jemima's own cottage), was virtually bare; certainly no one was hiding in there. Jemima saw twin beds, both empty, one with its blue cotton cover rumpled, the other untouched. She saw—

At that moment, the door behind slammed and all the lights in the cottage went out. Fumbling desperately in the darkness for the switch, Jemima found to her horror that she was grasping flesh, wet, clammy flesh, somewhere directly behind her. She screamed.

The light was switched on as suddenly as it had been extinguished. She was not touching flesh exactly, or not flesh unattached. What she was touching was a human hand.

"Why, Jemima Shore, I do declare!" exclaimed Fizzy in a palpable exaggeration of her usual drawl. "What the heck are you doing here?" She continued more briskly. "I saw someone going in. I guess I thought—I didn't know—"

"Where were you?" Fear and surprise had made Jemima angry; unreasonably so. Fizzy after all had a perfect right to come and go as she pleased in her own cottage. She added more politely by way of an explanation, "Your shutter was making rather a racket."

"Gee, I'm sorry." Fizzy looked down at herself. She was wearing a towelling robe, damp, and as it appeared not much else. "I've been treating myself to a late swim. I love to do that." She looked round the cottage. "I have some coffee in that thermos. Irini let me have it, she knows I'm a nocturnal animal. And I've an idea for a moonlight water-colour. Now how does one get to do that, do you suppose? Any ideas? Maybe Martha will advise. In the meantime, coffee?"

Jemima hesitated. "No, no, I've been enough trouble. Besides which, coffee keeps me awake. I won't stay." It was a decision she was to regret. Even at the time, she felt a pang at seeing how dashed Fizzy looked at the rejection of her offer.

Fizzy muttered something: "I'm not lonesome exactly but I do like to talk, nights. Have done ever since I was a kid." She was visibly disconsolate; Jemima had a touching vision of the kind of little girl Fizzy must have been, liking to "talk, nights" and maybe not getting all that many takers even then.

All the same, Jemima turned to go. Fizzy's last words reached her when her back was already set to the cottage. "And there's something special I'd like to talk to you about. But I guess the morning will do." It was too late to return: Jemima contented herself with a friendly wave of the defunct torch. Her last sight of the American girl was as she sketched a friendly salute back, still in her towelling robe, standing on her own terrace.

It was only after Jemima reached her own cottage that she realized she had not questioned Fizzy about the wailing on the beach. Had she heard it? She must have heard it if she had indeed been swimming. And if the wailing had existed in the first place.

Ah well, Jemima would make an opportunity to ask Fizzy about it first thing in the morning.

But Jemima never did make an opportunity to ask Fizzy about the subject in the morning. Because next morning at breakfast the whole scene was dominated by the discovery of the body; the sodden body lying on the beach at the edge of the water like a piece of abandoned wreckage, moving slowly from time to time with the sway of the sea, a dark and melancholy shape in the pristine sunshine of the bright new day.

The body, turning in the water at the edge of the sea, was first discovered by Irini's son Nikos, returning from one of his mysterious night-fishing expeditions.

Thank heaven, thought Jemima Shore, he had been there to do so. Otherwise one of the guests at the Villa Elia, taking an early-morning swim, might have happened upon it. For that respite at least they should all be devoutly thankful. It was illogical, the fact of death being as terrible and tragic whoever first stumbled upon the pathetic water-logged corpse. But in the circumstances Jemima was still grateful that it had not been anyone actually staying at the villa. They all needed to remain as calm and rational as possible if any sense was to be made of the whole horrifying business. To say nothing of when the local police arrived . . .

Quite early, Nikos had been heard calling from the beach to his mother up at the villa. It was a sound that for an instant gave Jemima a curious flash of recognition. Cry-by-night? Could that be the odd wailing noise which had disturbed Martha James and maybe awakened her too in the hours of darkness? Then the appalled expression of Sarah Halliwell swept these thoughts temporarily aside.

Sarah, who alone among the guests understood modern Greek, was listening to the shouts from the shore.

"He's saying—it's a *body*! Someone's in the water! He's saying—Kiria? No, I don't believe it!" Sarah swayed slightly and gripped one of the big terracotta pots at the edge of the terrace for support.

"Alice! He's telling his mother that it's *Alice* lying down there. There are injuries—her head. Something about the rocks!"

But it was the weeping, the terrible weeping and the stream of passionate but incomprehensible Greek lamentation from Irini, that brought it home to them all that Alice Garland was actually dead.

Irini raised her fists and looked up at the sky: the unclouded blue, the famous blue sky of Corfu, blue, Alice Garland's favourite colour, the theme of the Villa Elia, seemed to mock her. Too much blue in a house making for a heartless atmosphere, as Jemima's decorator friend Daisy had told her. Jemima had seen Alice herself as ruthless maybe in business, heartless perhaps in her private life (although she had greeted her disgraced husband's unexpected arrival with some generosity, pleading for his temporary acceptance in her little speech). Now Alice Garland was no longer in a position to be either ruthless or forgiving; only in a certain literal sense was she also heartless, for at some point in the small hours of the night, her heart had stopped beating.

"Little Alice!" began Fizzy in a voice of almost childish bewilderment; her heavy features crumpled and Jemima had the impression she was about to cry. "Why, no, you've gotta be joking." The words were in themselves ludicrous; yet at the same time what was happening, the macabre scene on the shore below them, was still so incredible to them all that it did cross Jemima's mind that maybe some hideous kind of practical joke was being played.

The arrival of William Gearhart on the terrace at this moment brought her back to a sense of reality—unwelcome reality. Irini, cries temporarily abandoned, was heading towards the path, apron askew, arms still outstretched. So far as Jemima knew, none of them had seen William since lunchtime the day before. Certainly she had not, and as for the others, that was something that could be checked, if not at the present moment.

William looked urbane and rested. The face was still rather flushed, perhaps, but the impression given this morning was of the flush of health, not the unhealthily ruddy hue of too much drink too often consumed. William was wearing a clean white tennis shirt and dark blue swimming trunks, despite the fact that he had arrived with no luggage: the shirt was slightly strained over his broad chest. Stock supplies at the villa? His own clothes left over from happier (and slimmer) times?

"Good morning, all." He not only looked, he sounded urbane. "I'm all ready for a fresh start this morning, a very fresh start except for the heat. My God, I'd forgotten the sheer delicious aroma of all those shrubs we planted—sage? I'm hopeless about names—as you make your way up the path. Fresh coffee now requested for a fresh start. Irini—" He stopped. "What's going on here? Irini, that's a hell of a racket. You all look as if someone had just died." The words faltered as he took in the shocked expression on Sarah's face.

Irini halted in mid-flight and grabbed William's hand.

"Kirie"—and she jabbered at him in Greek with gestures towards the shore. Someone had joined Nikos down there, another man, presumably Greek. Together they were lifting the body from the pebbles where Nikos had originally laid it and were heading, slowly, for the villa path.

"You poor thing!" said Mrs. Vascoe swiftly, before anyone else could interrupt. "I'm afraid this is going to be a terrible shock to you. But you see, we think there's been some kind of accident. Your wife—"

"Alice! No, I don't believe it." They were the words which Sarah Halliwell had spoken only a short while before. But William Gearhart, unlike Sarah, did not sway and needed no terracotta pot to support him. Nor was his voice low and gentle.

He began to shout, or perhaps rave might have been a better word. In his own way, William was almost as incomprehensible as Irini had been, or at least for the first few rapid sentences which he shouted at them. Then the words, to his appalled hearers—Fizzy, Sarah, Mrs. Vascoe and Jemima—did begin to make a certain grisly sense.

"Martha James!" was his recurrent theme. "Martha, Martha James! Why did you come here? Why didn't you leave her alone? Fatal Martha James! Fatal, fatal, fatal!" he shouted, his face getting redder by the minute; gone was the urbane new-that-morning-man entirely. "Unlucky to me. Unlucky to her. Martha James, where are you? Where are you lurking—? I know you, Martha James, fatal woman, where are you? Come out of your cottage." And on and on and on in a terrible stream of invective which on grounds of loudness alone could have been heard surely on the other side of the bay.

All the time the sombre little procession, body now wrapped round with some kind of dark towel or blanket or tarpaulin, could be seen winding its way up the path to the villa.

It was, oddly enough, William's mention of the word cottage, rather than his repeated vituperative evocation of her name, which called to everyone's attention the fact that Martha James was not actually present.

"She always came late for breakfast, she's always the last to come," said Sarah Halliwell when it was evident that for the time being William had worn himself to silence. She only put into words what the company as a whole was thinking.

"Then Martha doesn't *know*!" exclaimed Fizzy. "Maybe I

should go and tell her. I'd love to do something to *help*," she muttered pathetically. "This is gonna be such a shock: this terrible accident."

"Accident! Was it an accident?" To the general horror, William began to shout once more.

"Of course it was, dear Mr. Garland, Mr. Gearhart, rather." Mrs. Vascoe interposed her calming little voice. "A tragic accident, if your poor wife is indeed dead. As, alas, seems all too likely. What else could it be"—she quivered for a moment—"but an accident?"

"We shall see, I suppose." But William was subsiding once more; he spoke sombrely rather than with his previous rage.

"I'll get Martha then," put in Fizzy swiftly.

It was not necessary. Before Fizzy could move, Martha appeared on the terrace. Jemima noted that she was holding a lighted cigarette in her hand although she did not generally smoke before breakfast. One moment later, Nikos and his companion with their shrouded burden reached the crest of the path.

They all realized at once from the look of her that there was no need to tell Martha anything. She must have watched the procession coming up the path. Her face, like Irini's, was already streaked with tears. Before the mesmerized eyes of the assembled company—even William still mercifully silent—Martha sank on her knees beside Alice's body where it had been laid, and bowed her fair head down upon it. Even more shocking was the way she burrowed in the dark covering to produce one white moist hand and some strands of long wet hair.

Martha James proceeded to kiss the hand of the dead girl with passionate abandonment as the tears flowed freely down her cheeks. "My Alice! Little Alice!" After a while she stayed silent and simply bowed herself once more over the corpse.

"Did she mean *that* to you too?" Fizzy spoke with a sort of awe. "But I guess we all loved her," she added generously.

Then Jemima looked at Martha, looked at her again with new eyes: saw the straight, fairish hair hanging down her back, framing the curiously wizened face with its unexpected crop of lines fanning out beneath the deepening tan; Martha's girlish hair-style and Martha's girlish slimness. Girlish from a distance, that is. Yes. But Martha James was not the girl, that was Alice Garland. Jemima looked away from Martha down to Alice's prostrate form, the pale wet mermaid hair now falling free from its covering in strands; she imagined the pale face beneath.

Martha and Alice: "My Alice! Little Alice!" She thought of William's uncontrolled railing against Martha, as yet imperfectly understood. Might that hatred have its true origin in the most primitive kind of jealousy and dislike?

Jemima stepped forward and touched Martha on the shoulder.

"I think I understand," was all she said. Then, putting her arm protectively round Martha's shoulder, Jemima helped her to her feet and away from the body of the dead girl. She decided to say nothing further for the time being.

"Well, *I* don't understand." Fizzy's voice was loud, indignant, her expression, again childlike, a mixture of misery and crossness. "I don't understand at all. We're talking about an accident, aren't we? Of course we are. But how did she die? I want to know that. Are we getting the doctor? I've got a lot of questions to ask." She glared about her; her lip trembled.

"My dear Fizzy." Mrs. Vascoe spoke gently. "We all know what you mean, I'm sure. We've all got a lot of questions to ask. And for that matter, I expect one or two questions will be asked of us. In the meantime, surely we must all be as cooperative and *self-controlled* as possible." Mrs. Vascoe put an unmistakable emphasis on the last words.

Sarah nodded strongly. So did William. It was clear that he did not consider the words could possibly apply to him.

There was no telephone at the Villa Elia. Telephones were hard to get in Corfu it seemed (and precarious when they were installed). Jemima remembered with a pang how Alice had spoken merrily on the subject: "One of the many good points of the villa. When you come to film it, you'll find it so peaceful without a telephone. Not really very awkward once you adjust to it. For urgent calls, you just go up to the village and chance your luck. Now that really is a time-wasting experience. Most people decide to make their fresh start *without* the benefit of the telephone."

You might have thought, however, that a telephone would be sadly missed in the present unhappy circumstances. But Irini's force of character and organizational abilities, with Nikos as her aide, and Nikos's friend as *his* aide, proved able to cope with, under the circumstances, surprising dispatch. Alice's body was taken to a small room on the ground floor, a bare, cell-like little place, but that seemed right enough. Irini had ceased her keening now that she had something—in fact a great deal—to do.

A doctor arrived, Greek but English-speaking, accompanied by a man who appeared to be the local policeman.

From the doctor it was learned what they perfectly well knew already, but he insisted on pronouncing the news officially—that Alice Garland was dead. But they also learned—the assembled company was once more on the terrace—that Alice had died not from drowning, but from a blow or blows on the side of the head. From a stone? A rock? How many blows? The doctor, having given them this news, was not inclined to elaborate upon it.

In short, and this was the key-point of his announcement: Alice Garland had been dead before she entered the water.

"She fell? Yes, maybe she has fallen. Maybe a big rock has fallen on her. The rocks do fall in this bay. They are loose a bit, do you know. Then she fell in the water. But I think she was dead, then. Already dead, I do not think she did drown. We shall know more." He paused diplomatically. He means, Jemima supposed, after the autopsy; but he is too delicate to conjure up such a distressing image in our minds.

The policeman spoke limited English, and so that the tenor of his remarks could be clearly understood Sarah Halliwell translated them. The message, although given at some length, causing Sarah to pause once or twice and hesitate for the right official word, was in essence a simple one.

None of the guests was free to leave the villa until further formalities—further questioning was another way of putting it—had taken place.

"He wants our passports, I think: to look at them," murmured Sarah with a shade of embarrassment. "And he also wants to know the answer to two questions immediately. I'm not sure—I'd better just pass them on."

"Go on, for God's sake! Tell us what he's saying! Don't start holding things back at this stage." William Gearhart had been trying to follow the conversation with obvious impatience. It was clear that unlike Alice (who had spoken excellent modern Greek) William knew very little of the language.

"First of all," said Sarah in a stronger voice, sounding defiant, "he wants to know who is now in charge of this party at the Villa Elia."

There was a silence which nobody seemed inclined to break.

"And the second question?" inquired William harshly.

"He wants to know who is the next of kin of the unfortunate lady. As he describes her, Alice."

"I can answer both of those questions. Together." William exuded a deep breath. "I am, was, *am*, Alice's lawful husband. She had not so far as I know changed her will, in spite of our—separation. So I inherit the villa. The same goes for her next of kin. I'm still her husband. Legally, which is what counts. So, QED, I'm still her next of kin."

"Nonsense," rapped out Martha James sharply. "That's absolute nonsense, William. Alice *had* changed her will. I know that for a fact. You won't inherit the villa, and Alice, as you know, had at the moment of her death nothing much else to leave."

"And I suppose you *will* inherit it? Is that what you're trying to say?" William's tone was sarcastic rather than serious.

"Exactly." Martha dragged on her cigarette. "Quite appropriate, don't you think? In view of everything."

"But how could that be?" cried Fizzy in great agitation. "You? You meant nothing to her. You were just her business partner. You were handling those antiques with her. I know all about it. Nikos was shipping them out for her, with the help of some other friends. She wanted to build it up. She lost a lot of money when *you*"—she looked angrily at William—"let her down. People were always letting her down. But *she* was into helping people—like Nikos for example!" Fizzy turned back to Martha. "You were just an old friend, down on your luck, she was helping you to make a fresh start."

"An old friend!" Martha bent her sardonic gaze on the American girl; Fizzy, alone of them all, had attempted some kind of adjustment of her dress to indicate grief or at least mourning: she had wrapped a scrubby black scarf round her head; the effect was to recall the seventies' protests against the Vietnam War rather than bereavement in the eighties. All the same, Jemima thought that it revealed a tenderness in Fizzy which so far no one else, not William, the self-styled bereaved husband, nor Martha, had attempted to exhibit.

"An old friend!" repeated Martha. "Yes, you could put it like that."

"I don't want to speak out of turn," Mrs. Vascoe began with the habitual note of apology in her voice and ended more briskly. "This is all very distasteful under the circumstances. But perhaps you should know now, as you don't seem to be aware—in short, poor Alice and I were partners. We'd gone into partnership over Fresh Perspectives. The villa, the whole business. I'd been thinking about doing something useful since Harry died; he would have wanted me to do something useful, I know he would. Alice and I discussed it. She needed the capital. You know about that, Mr. Gearhart. That was my fresh start, it is my fresh start." She gazed firmly round. "If anyone is in control here now, and I don't want to obtrude too much of course, but I really think, Martha, Mr. Gearhart, it must be"—she paused as if struggling against the apology trying to return to her voice—"well, me."

"This is not distasteful, as you put it, it's horrible!" burst out Fizzy. "Poor little Alice, hardly cold yet." She shuddered. "We don't even know how she died, and we're quarrelling over business. Didn't you care for her at all?"

"It must be obvious even to you, Fizzy, that some of us cared for her a great deal," Martha countered.

It was suddenly unbearably hot and the happy cries from the far side of the bay—the tourists had come with the noonday sun—were increasingly obtrusive to the tense group on the terrace above.

"How like Alice! Even now we're all quarrelling over her. I told you it was a mistake." Surprisingly this bitter exclamation came from Sarah Halliwell. What was more, it was to William Gearhart that she turned as she said it.

"You mean: I shouldn't have come? I had to come. You know that I had to see you."

"Hey! Are you guys serious? Is this some kind of love scene you're gonna play out?" Fizzy was now more truculent than bewildered. Jemima, feeling herself to be the outsider in this increasingly murky discussion, judged it the moment to intervene.

"Shouldn't we all step back from this a little?" she queried in her most reasonable voice, the one she kept in reserve for battling interviewees in her investigative television series. "We've all had a shock, a number of shocks as a matter of fact. Obviously this wasn't just a normal Fresh Perspective house party, to put it mildly. You two, Sarah and William, obviously know each other; Martha was a close and old *friend*"—she emphasized the word deliberately without looking at the painter—"of Alice. Fizzy, you were a new, newish friend?"

Fizzy nodded strongly.

"Mrs. Vascoe, you were her partner, new, newish partner?"

Mrs. Vascoe inclined her head.

"What is quite obvious to me," went on Jemima, "if rather too late in the day, is that Alice Garland wasn't content for me to make up my own mind about the value or otherwise of Fresh Perspectives. She was sufficiently keen on my using some film of it for television to ensure that my visit was in a sense rigged. Mrs. Vascoe, you would talk about your late husband." Jemima smiled nicely in her direction. "Fizzy, you would talk about your bad marriage." Another smile, polite, not quite so nice. "Sarah, I'm not sure about you. You mentioned a personal betrayal, perhaps you really were here getting a fresh perspective on things. Yet you clearly know Alice's estranged husband well."

But Sarah Halliwell chose neither to confirm nor to deny what Jemima had said.

It was William Gearhart who burst out, with something of a return to his original intemperate manner, "Of course we know each other. And there was a betrayal, a highly personal betrayal. But the betrayer was Alice, not me. I'd like to make that absolutely clear. Alice used her knowledge in the gallery, quoted her, got her name involved. When I went up the spout, Sarah lost her job."

"William," broke in Sarah, "do we have to have all this out again? And in public? It's nothing to do with poor Alice's death. She offered me the trip to make up, I suppose. She was generous, she could be generous. And yes, Jemima, you're right. Alice did ask us all along to make up a convincing party for you, even though our reasons for a fresh start were, speaking of myself, perfectly genuine ones."

"Nothing to do with Alice's death?" hissed Fizzy. "That's for the police to say, I think. How do we know it *was* an accident? You were out and about last night, Sarah Halliwell. I saw you all right when I took my dip. I saw the light in your cottage, saw it come on, you were there moving about. Who's to say you didn't go up to the house, lure poor little Alice down to the shore . . ." She broke off, even Fizzy aware that she might, just might, be going too far.

"I have no intention of denying that I left my cottage last night." Sarah spoke proudly. "As a matter of fact, I visited William's cottage. I reasoned with him. I tried to persuade him to leave in the morning. There was nothing to be gained from being here. The past was the past: there was nothing more either of us could do about it. Right, William?"

"Perfectly right. Why not add that we spent the night together? That we made love, if you prefer to put it that way. So unless Fizzy is going to accuse us *both* of lying, and *both* of murdering Alice, I think this delightful young woman must really accept—"

"Are you patronizing me? I don't buy that," Fizzy threatened him. But the word "murder," mentioned for the first time, cast a new and frightful shadow on all of them.

It was the re-emergence of Irini, weeping once more now that there was temporarily no need for her executive qualities and expostulating in Greek—the word Nikos could be heard repeatedly—which put an end to the whole distressing scene.

"Poor Irini, and still more poor Nikos," sighed Sarah at the end of it all. "Nikos is wondering what is going to happen to him, or rather what is going to happen to the business."

Mrs. Vascoe smiled eagerly. "Oh, please, do assure them, Sarah, I wish I knew some Greek, I've been boning up, but I don't know enough yet to say something as important as this. So you must assure them on my behalf that of course the business will go on, of course Irini won't lose her job! Hardly. She's the mainstay. As for Nikos, I'm not quite clear exactly what he does, but whatever arrangement Alice had made with him, I'll surely honour that. Harry taught me to have everything very clear from the start, and I certainly mean to get everything clear from now on—"

Sarah was looking at her with some embarrassment; then she silently raised an eyebrow in William's direction. He nodded.

"Mrs. Vascoe, this is going to be quite embarrassing, I fear. But the business which Irini is worrying about, Nikos's business with Alice, is the one Fizzy mentioned to you. Rather too blithely, I'm afraid, under the circumstances. We have reason to believe that Alice was shipping out certain antiquities—vases—using Nikos." She stopped.

"Now you listen here"—Fizzy, belligerent once more. "Alice may no longer be here to protect herself, but that's no reason why the whole of this should be dumped on her.

What about you, Martha? It was your idea: Alice told me that. There were some odd things going on up at your cottage, I know it. Some restoring, painting up. I took a look one day. Jemima, I wanted to talk to you about that, last night. You went away."

Irini said something very fierce in Greek to Sarah and threw her hands up in the air once more. Then she stalked off the terrace back in the direction of the kitchen.

"What did she say, Sarah?" asked Mrs. Vascoe. "I don't know what to think. What would Harry think? Is it true?"

"She says she wishes Kiria Alice had never tried to make the Villa Elia into a business, never involved Nikos in business; she says Kiria Alice and Kirie William were happy once together when they built the villa."

"I was happy. Alice was never really happy. She could never leave anything or anyone alone. No sooner did we build that villa than she saw how it could be used. The gallery too, that could be used."

On that sad little speech, spoken at last with resignation rather than rage, William Gearhart turned away. His slumped figure could be seen wandering back in the direction of his cottage. After a moment Sarah shrugged her shoulders and followed him. It was a signal for the rest of the party to disperse, Fizzy allowing herself one Parthian shot: "When the police start to ask the real questions, there'll be some explaining to do."

A long swim must be in order, thought Jemima, in the late afternoon. There was no sign of the doctor, nor the local policeman, no kind of official had come near them since the last incursion. Were they all to spend another night together then? Under the general unhappy umbrella of the stricken villa? That seemed to be the general plan, or rather, in the general lack of plan (no outside touring office to assist them: Alice had *been* the office), there did not appear to be any alternative. To remove oneself to a hotel—always supposing one was to be found empty in the high tourist season—might be tactless under the circumstances.

In the afternoon a grim-faced Irini did reappear: she visited Jemima's cottage and was on her way to the others. Nikos had been, she learnt, up at the police station, but was now back. There was nothing sinister about his presence there, Jemima understood. So far. She did not know what the ramifications of Alice's death would be for Nikos—his friends—and their presumably illegal smuggling business. The message Irini brought to her, written in careful English, was that officialdom would return to the Villa Elia tomorrow.

Another night together! Not dinner together, surely? That would be too much. But no, Irini was going up to the village: there was nothing for her to do here but mourn; Irini mimed sorrow. Another note, written in much less good but still comprehensible English, indicated that Irini's sister would prepare a cold supper and leave it for them all as usual on the terrace. After that it was up to the individuals concerned to eat it there, or carry it away to their separate cottages.

A long swim was definitely in order. Picking her way carefully along the pretty but stony beach, Jemima avoided the spot where Alice's body had been found. It was marked—by Nikos? by Nikos at Irini's orders? by the police? by Fizzy?—by a little cairn of stones.

Once she was in the sea, Jemima floated out easily into the bay. The water grew deep within a few yards of the shore; the swell was gentle but commanding, the water almost chilly. (Even in high summer the Corfu water, unlike that of the rest of Greece, remained coolish and thus invigorating.) Jemima turned on her back and looked back at the villa itself, the cliffs and headlands, the extensive olive-spattered territories of the Villa Elia. The little cairn remained a marker and a monument which she had to admit could not be ignored.

How peaceful and clean everything looked now, washed in the late afternoon sun! Yet it was this very shore which on the night of Alice's death—without any knowledge of what was occurring—had seemed to Jemima so abruptly menacing, cries heard, lights perhaps flickering, a boat maybe seen. Had it been her instinct that something evil was afoot? A fatal accident: that was after all a far more likely explanation. Why had William, and Fizzy too, seemed to jump to the conclusion that there was something unnatural, as well as tragic, about what had happened?

Fresh starts, fresh perspectives. Lapped by the water, gazing up at the villa itself (blue shutters now firmly closed against sun—or tragedy), Jemima began to meditate anew on the so-called theme of the Villa Elia holidays.

Supposing Alice had been killed? Presumably they would know for sure in the morning. Had she been killed to prevent her making a fresh start? Or in revenge by those incapable of making one? Fizzy might come into the first category, or even Martha, locked in their jealousy of each other; William and Sarah in the second. Mrs. Vascoe, on the other hand, if as innocent as she seemed about Alice's secret smuggling ventures, had no motive to wish the dead woman ill. But if Mrs. Vascoe was a somewhat deeper character than she appeared—not altogether improbable, since she had surprised them all with her news of the partnership—then she might have got hold of some inkling of Alice's business-within-a-business. And she might not have liked what she found out, the misuse of her money, the misuse of the late Harry's money . . . Under these circumstances, even meek little Betsy Vascoe might find it in her nature to behave less like an apologetic mouse and more like an enraged rat.

Jemima watched as a figure, a woman, walked along the shore and paused by the small cairn, her head bowed. From her figure, so much more substantial than that of the rest of the female guests, Jemima guessed she was looking at Fizzy. She saw the black scarf fluttering round her head. At this distance, Fizzy looked both fine and dignified.

Fizzy? No, Fizzy could not have desired Alice's death. Fizzy had manifestly hero-worshipped Alice. Jemima remembered the embarrassing spectacle of some of Fizzy's enthusiasms; how graceful Alice Garland had dealt with them, used them as it now seemed. Surely Fizzy could never have wished for any harm to come to Alice, her model of all a woman should be, practical, helpful, businesslike . . . Jemima recalled Fizzy's frequent outbursts of praise.

Martha, then? How could Martha have desired Alice's death? Other words rang in Jemima's ears: Martha's words. "My Alice." And then Fizzy's further exclamation: "All our pasts are crying out to haunt us." The figure of Fizzy, head still bowed, had by now walked away from the cairn, and vanished among the olive trees.

A fresh perspective . . . wait. Jemima saw suddenly how you might look at the whole matter from another angle; she began instinctively to swim back for the shore with a practised crawl that was very different from the reflective way she had been floating, and looking up at the villa. Then she realized that there was in fact no hurry for what she had to do. She swam more slowly, floating again. Night would fall and with it the gentle cloak of warm darkness which would cover all things and make them, at least for the time being, acceptable.

A confession. Jemima thought that there had been enough pain already, and enough shame; more pain, if not more shame, might be avoided if certain things were known, confessed, before the officials came in the morning.

"You did care for her," she said much later that night, sitting on the terrace of the other person's cottage; "I know that. You cared for her most of all. And so you killed her."

"Would you believe me if I told you it was an accident?" The person spoke in a low voice. Both of them looked out to sea. The cottage was in darkness. There were no lights on the terrace. Both had preferred it that way.

"In a way it was an accident. I wanted her to let me go. Why couldn't she let me make a fresh start?"

"But you never could," Jemima spoke gently. "You were the one person who could never make a fresh start while Alice Garland was alive. And perhaps not now, now that she's dead."

"When did you guess?"

"The one bond that can't be broken, ignored, forgotten. That's it, isn't it? That's what kept you as her slave?"

"The bond was—"

"Motherhood. That was it, wasn't it?" Silence fell. "Alice Garland was your daughter, wasn't she? That was the hold she had over you. The hold that meant she would never let you go."

Martha James's cigarette glowed in the darkness. Jemima could see a little white heap of stubs in the pottery ashtray—blue like everything else—at her feet.

"I knew when you knelt by her body. You looked so alike. Even at that moment."

"No fresh start for me," said Martha James. "Not while

Alice was alive. You're right. I realized that at last. I realized it in fact last night."

"I think you must have fought with her," continued Jemima. "You must have suffered so much: being involved yet again in one of her crooked businesses. She used you: you *had* to be loyal to her. She'd used you, I imagine, over the gallery business, as she'd used William and Sarah Halliwell. As she was now using Fizzy, poor, hapless, devoted creature, and Mrs. Vascoe. Your reputation had already suffered. Now she was going to use you all over again, restoring, painting up, as Fizzy euphemistically put it. Finally, I suppose"—she hesitated—"I suppose your loyalty came to an end."

"I did fight with her," admitted Martha. "I was haunted by those cries: at first I did think it was some kind of a ghost, a woman wailing, the woman I had been, if you like, an expression of my conscience. But that night, *last* night, for God's sake, I began to understand a little more of how she operated. Nikos and the boat, devoted Nikos, so eager to work up his own little business, trusting her that she would not get him into trouble. Loyalty—where was *her* loyalty? Those cries were Nikos's signal. For the loading, I imagine.

"I heard the cries. I went out. Nikos was leaving the boat. No wailing woman, but plenty of bad conscience; she had me looking at the vases, restoring all day. Now the results were being shipped off. I should never have indulged her, spoiled her, helped her. William knew that; hence his outburst. Justified in a sort of ghastly way, I suppose. I was unlucky to her. Alice always wanted something more, you know. With her little angel's face, she could wheedle anyone. Beginning with her mother."

"Beginning: but not ending."

"Not ending. No. Last night I hit her. I'd never done that

before, not even when she was a little girl. I didn't believe in it: ironic, isn't it? But last night she laughed at me; said the only value of my work was to make a little money for her. Laughed at me for thinking the world had lost anything with the failure of Martha James, artist. 'You can't escape me, ever, you're my mother, you're not a painter, you're my mother.' That was when my loyalty ended, if you like. Or my control. Listening to her laughter. 'You're not a painter, you're my mother.' Her last words. I went towards her: I slapped her, hard, she fell, she stumbled, we were on the little path, on the edge of the cliff, she fell.

"I ran down," went on Martha. "She had fallen, fallen all the way. She was dead. No pulse, nothing. There must be—injuries. The doctor will tell you about that. Her head had hit a rock. I never meant to kill her."

"You were quite sure she was dead?"

"Of course," replied Martha in her cool, spare manner; the emotion had drained from her voice; they might have been discussing, once more, the fishing boats, the stars or the night breeze. "She was dead. And so I floated her body out to sea. Mad: I was mad. I had killed the person I loved, and so I let her float away in the water. The cleansing water."

"But Alice floated back." Jemima kept her voice equally lacking in emotion.

"She came back to me. Yet again. There was to be no escape, as she had told me, no fresh start for *me*. I'll tell them all this in the morning, of course. The others will know too. They'll recover. Fizzy will find someone else to hero-worship. William and Sarah have each other. Mrs. Vascoe: she'll find something more truly useful to do. But for me"—Martha James stared out in the darkness as though she could still see her daughter's body floating on the edge of the sea—"there isn't any escape from her, from Alice, ever."

Jemima put out her hand and gently touched the older woman's thin brown arm. She thought that what Martha had said was probably true: for this particular mother there could never be a real escape.

Aloud, all she said was, "You didn't really want that, Martha, did you? Up to the end, you wanted to protect her: she was your little girl."

7
DEAD LEAVES

The first thing I noticed was the leaves. Or rather the lack of them. The deep ocean of dry brown leaves which had settled over the Jarvis forecourt in October and had remained there untouched for so many weeks—it was now late November—had suddenly been removed. Or at least partly removed, in the corner which I could see. Normally I would have been delighted. I hate disorder and the sight of this dead ocean offended me. But things weren't normal. That meant, had to mean, that Galina Jarvis was back. And so my heart sank when I thought of Marcus. It would be the first thing Galina did, the very first thing she did, to sweep the leaves away from the forecourt: advertising to the world—and to Marcus—that she was back.

And sure enough, when I went upstairs and got a better view out of my bedroom window there was Galina Jarvis herself, wearing her cherry-red woollen hat, the one she always wore to keep her warm during the leaf-sweeping. She'd only made a start on all the leaves she had to move.

Politely enough—Galina always had good manners, if you like, except where men and money were concerned—she'd started at the corner nearest my house. It was going to take her some time.

Later the police told me that it was also the last thing she did: that sweeping.

Behind the huge pile of black plastic sacks already full of leaves in the far corner of the forecourt, Galina's body was found. She hadn't quite finished the job. There were still some leaves underneath and around her body. The postman noticed her red hat the next morning and went to investigate. She still wore the cherry-red woollen hat. The key to the house was in her pocket. She was clutching the broom in her cold hand, Galina Jarvis, beautiful in life, but perhaps not so beautiful in death (I never actually asked the police how she looked), had been brutally beaten with her own spade many times.

The detective in charge of the case did tell me that the first blow would have been enough.

"Enough for the deceased, that is, poor lady. Not enough for him. The murderer, I mean. He really went to town on this one."

"A man then?" I enquired delicately.

"A man and a strong one at that. If you can show me a woman with that kind of strength, even these days, whatever *they* say—"

It was not clear exactly who *they* were, but I got the impression that the detective was making some confused protest against the growth of women's liberation. As I agreed with him (why advertise ourselves when we've been managing things perfectly well for centuries?) I did not pursue the point. As a matter of fact the late Galina Jarvis would have agreed with him too, her approach to men and life having been distinctly old-fashioned.

"No, not a woman's crime, not a brutal beating like this. A man and a young one, if you want my opinion."

"I'm glad I'm in the clear at least, Inspector," I said modestly. "On two counts what is more. Age and sex."

Inspector Portsmouth smiled and patted my knee: a gesture to which I suppose he thought I was entitled by my advancing years.

"Oh, Mrs. Langhorn, it would never do for us to go about suspecting sweet little old ladies like you. Besides you're just the sort of person who solves the problem in the murder stories my wife reads. Says they take her mind off my work, whatever that means."

I smiled in my turn: graciously, I like to think.

"Don't forget, Inspector, I'm a witness as well. About the leaves and the timing, I mean. I can be quite exact about that. I passed down the side of the Square at one o'clock because the Sub Post Office closes for lunch at one-fifteen. Such nice people there now! The Singhs. We have experiences in Kenya in common. Now don't smile: it does form a bond, even if mine were safaris in the thirties with my late husband, and hers were—well, rather different. I certainly appreciate their arrival in our little neighborhood. To return to the leaves: as I passed, there was Galina Jarvis sweeping up her leaves. And I said as much to Mrs. Singh behind the counter. 'Mrs. Jarvis is back,' I observed. "It had to be one-fifteen, when they close.

"After that I went shopping, went to the hairdresser—I still like to keep myself nice. I had a cup of coffee and a pastry in the new so-called Viennese place: a little treat if you like after the hairdresser. I was back at six: I know the time because I popped into the Singhs' shop for a *Standard* on my way. It was quite dark of course. There was no way I could have noticed—" I hesitated. "Her," I said finally.

"We certainly know the leaves were thick in the morning," commented the Inspector. "Both neighbours—the houses on either side, numbers thirty-five and thirty-seven—swear the leaves were untouched when they went to work in the morning. 'Desolate-looking,' Cavett, the City man at number thirty-five, called it. 'Had been for at least a month.' He was surprised no one had tried to burgle the house he said: such an advertisement for its being empty. His own house is actually for sale but he's still right there on the site; the result is that everyone thinks the Jarvis house is the one for sale because of the leaves."

"No crime while she was away," I commented thoughtfully, "and then a major crime the moment she came back. No matter that she lost her life as a result of it: that's no excuse. Inspector, I must tell you plainly that Galina Jarvis was a trouble-maker all her life, and this is the final proof." I think the Inspector looked rather startled at this point of view: he certainly didn't pat my knee again after what I said.

I should tell you about the leaves. All our houses in Notting Square have these wide paved areas in front of them. Forecourts, we call them, although that does sound rather like a garage, doesn't it, something most inappropriate to Notting Square, designed as it was in the Regency period and still elegantly looking it. The forecourts are not gardens, at any rate, but an area behind the high railings which sets each house back from the road. We have our gardens, of course, beautiful gardens too, but they lie behind the houses, tucked well out of sight.

Some of us put a couple of bay trees in the forecourt, and there is one bed of floribunda roses—not quite appropriate, I sometimes think. I myself have one very large magnolia which I planted when my grandson Marcus was born nearly thirty years ago. Nothing really softens the fact that these are rather dreary dark forecourts. They are merely intended to distance the busy world yet another fifteen yards from the discreet silent houses of Notting Square, with its huge leafy trees, above us and protecting us all.

Then in the autumn the leaves come. For weeks they torrent relentlessly down on top of us, floating, hurtling, scudding, according to the weather. Fast or slow, they still keep on coming down. There's no avoiding them. The Council, in the shape of some reluctant men in blue overalls, do sweep the leaves off the streets, in a manner of speaking, into the black plastic bags, and after a week or two—too long in my opinion—take them away. But we're responsible for our own forecourts.

To tell the truth I rather like sweeping up the leaves. It's not a hard job. I have my own little broom based on my own pint size (to which Inspector Portsmouth alluded with such heavy-handed gallantry), and the fact that you have to do the sweeping all over again the next day, and the next, and the next after that, gives the job a certain timeless quality. Marcus, my grandson, who lives in the basement flat of my house, is supposed to do things like sweeping the leaves for me. As he's supposed to do other heavy jobs which I can't manage. But as a matter of fact, I sometimes wryly reflect, it's nearly always exactly the other way round. The truth is, I *like* bringing order into chaos, and you can't exactly say that about Marcus. There'll be plenty of time for him to change his ways, plenty of time before I'm really frail. Besides, it has to be admitted that when you sweep a forecourt, you see what's going on in the world, don't you?

For example, it was while at my sweeping, a year ago last October—rather early in the morning, but then I do like to get going early—that I realized my grandson Marcus was spending his nights with Galina Jarvis. Those nights, that is, she was not spending with her rich Spanish admirer, the one who visits her in the Mercedes car, sometimes with the chauffeur, sometimes without. And it was during my sweeping *this* year in late September—a quick foray as you might say to catch the early ones, the forerunners before the main army drops from the sky—that I established how and with whom Galina Jarvis departed for her holiday.

She went, of course, with the Spaniard. To be frank, who else could afford to keep Galina in the luxury she demanded? Of her current admirers, that is. Not Marcus certainly; for Marcus I fear belongs to another army, the kind of army which doesn't so much drop from the sky as lie around in the streets, or in Marcus's case on my sofa—the army of the unemployed. No wonder Marcus gets depressed sometimes: I urge him—generally—to go down to the gym and work it off, to the gym not the pub.

Nor could Charlie Jarvis, Galina's unfortunate husband, afford to take her on holiday: Galina had already ruined *him*, I fear, with her gaily insouciant extravagance. Poor Charlie Jarvis: no wonder he hates her, hated her I should say, for in his case Galina ruined him but somehow kept the house, the splendid freehold house in Notting Square. Charlie Jarvis was born in that house: he always loved it, even as a rumbustious little boy. And now he's in a tiny flat, a bedsitter, I believe. Except he has to be local for his new office in Kensington High Street, it might have been better to move just a little further away. Altogether too poignant. For it seems our freeholds are worth a fortune these days, or so they tell me: irrelevant information in my case, for I was born in Notting Square too, you know, and with any luck will die in it. Except I don't want to die alone, of course: so "with any luck" means that I hope Marcus will still be here to "look after" me.

"Oh, Mrs. Langhorn, you're not to go talking about dying like that," said Mrs. Singh to me, when I observed something along these lines to her. "I am sure Marcus is not thinking like that too," she added in her kindly way. "He is loving his old granny." For Mrs. Singh of course knows all about Marcus. She probably knows all about Marcus and Galina Jarvis too—knew about them, I should say. Mrs. Singh certainly knows that I'm depending on Marcus to take care of me—when the time comes and I can no longer manage to take care of him.

I never told Marcus what I saw that September morning: first of all Galina with her expensive suitcases, brand names stamped all over them. (Now that is vulgar! Or would have been in my day.) Then the Spaniard, acting discreetly in his terms, maybe, as he stole out of the house: he did look to left and right, and the collar of his camelhair coat was turned up; all the same he couldn't resist a kiss, a quick kiss on her soft cheek, her soft plump cheek, as they stole out of the house together.

(How *did* she look when she was dead? But I don't think I can ask the police, not under the circumstances.)

Of course I didn't tell Marcus what I saw. Just as I didn't tell Marcus she had returned. I think Inspector Portsmouth believed me; he certainly asked me about it enough times: Marcus's relationship with Galina, Marcus's feelings for Galina, even the break-up of Marcus's relationship with Galina. Ah well, as I told Inspector Portsmouth, that's past history.

"Mrs. Langhorn," said the Inspector patiently, "you do realize that your evidence of the timing is crucial? We've been over this before—" We had indeed. Many times. "I need not remind a lady of your—" What word was he going to use? "A lady of your seniority," he continued with a smile, "of the importance of precision in a case like this."

No, he certainly did not need to remind me of its importance: for I was quite as well aware as Inspector Portsmouth that Marcus had an unimpeachable alibi for the lunchtime period. That is to say, he'd been in the pub, our local as a matter of fact, where he's rather well known. He arrived at twelve-thirty, plenty of witnesses to that, and left at closing time, about three, having eaten a pub lunch and drunk quite a few drinks. Then he went to the cinema up at Notting Hill Gate, plenty of witnesses to that because he goes quite often in the afternoon; it was almost empty and as a result the usherette swears he didn't leave till five o'clock, in the Inspector's words, "No crafty slipping out to the Gents." He sat on the opposite side of the cinema and never moved from his seat. While five o'clock—the time of his return—is too late for the time of death.

"So, Mrs. Langhorn, if you saw Galina Jarvis sweeping the leaves away at one o'clock—"

"I did, Inspector," I said firmly. "I'm quite clear about that. Just as I mentioned the fact to Mrs. Singh, and she's quite clear about that too."

"The money, Mrs. Langhorn," the Inspector went on rather more abruptly. He was beginning to drop the gallantry, I noted, and no longer treated me as a little old lady, more as an adversary. "You gave your grandson some money to go to the pub. And some money to go to the cinema. Wasn't that rather an odd thing to do? When you have told several people round here you don't approve of Marcus going to the pub."

"Odd?" I frowned in what I hoped looked like genuine puzzlement. "The poor boy *has* no money—"

"Yes, perhaps it wasn't so odd. Is it possible, Mrs. Langhorn, you were determined your grandson should be out of the way for a particular period, say twelve-thirty to four, and that was one way of making sure? But of course if Galina Jarvis, *seen only by you,* was not alive at one o'clock, was already dead before twelve-thirty—"

"Seen only by me, Inspector? Oh, whatever gave you that

idea? Oh, no, no, no. Mrs. Singh saw Mrs. Jarvis. Didn't she tell you? You know what they're like about the police, don't quite trust them sometimes, I fear. She'll tell you now, I'm sure. When I told her Mrs. Jarvis was back, she was reminded that Mrs. Jarvis hadn't paid her bill, rather a big one, cigarettes, magazines, papers, going back months, back to the time she tricked Charlie Jarvis out of the house. 'Mrs. Singh,' I said, 'you'll catch her now if you run up the hill. She's there sweeping the leaves in that cherry-red hat of hers.' And sure enough she did, the moment she closed for lunch. So she saw Galina Jarvis: I'm afraid she didn't get a cheque though. 'Not a convenient time, Mrs. S.,' said Galina in her languid way, with the broom in her hand. Poor Mrs. Singh could hardly insist: they're so polite. And now—" I maintained discreet silence. Frankly I thought it unlikely that any of the three men connected with the late Galina Jarvis would pay up for her, not the Spaniard, not Marcus—and not Charlie Jarvis. Not Charlie, even though Charlie had now of course regained possession of his beloved house, Galina having made no will while the divorce settlement was in the process of being thrashed out.

So it will be Charlie Jarvis sweeping up the dead leaves at number 36 next year: in theory at least. Of course he may be engaged in some rather different form of menial work, or exercising in a rather different form of courtyard. How long will it take the police to reach Charlie Jarvis, I wonder? I don't feel inclined to help them any further, I'm afraid, especially in view of Inspector Portsmouth's recent quite unpleasantly abrupt manner. Besides, I have sometimes been accused of being quite a nagging person—all things considered, I think I'll keep out of the affairs of the late Galina Jarvis in future.

Let Inspector Portsmouth reach the obvious conclusion concerning Charlie Jarvis himself, now he's got rid of this silly obsession about my grandson Marcus and all those threats he was heard making about Galina and the Spaniard.

"When she comes back, I'll fix her." That sort of thing, spread about the pub, I believe. So stupid and reckless. No wonder I had to do something about it all, and quickly, when I saw that Galina was back. Because I need Marcus, you see, I need him to look after me in the future, here at the end of my life in Notting Square.

As for Charlie Jarvis, I doubt whether he will think it wise to tell the police about that telephone call. He'll be in too much trouble trying to explain away what happened when he got there. I think it was the sight of the for sale board on the railings of his house that actually did it. Just a quick telephone call to Charlie Jarvis and a word in his ear that Galina had come back with her nice Spanish friend and did he know that she had just put the house up for sale? I've always kept in touch with him, you see, so I had his telephone number handy. After he had to move to that flat, I really think he enjoyed my little reports on the progress of the Square garden—that sort of thing. That was my only part in it all, such a very minor one. I simply don't think the Inspector need be bothered with it. By the time they'd had a flaming row it was too late for Charlie Jarvis to realize that it was actually the house next door that was for sale.

How *many* blows? He was always such a violent little boy, a terror at Marcus's parties, I remember it well. But I mustn't think about that too much.

"Now you will be taking great care of yourself, Mrs. Langhorn," said Mrs. Singh this morning. "Marcus too. He must take care of his granny."

"He will, Mrs. Singh, he will," I replied. "After all, I've taken great care of him."

8
OUT FOR
THE COUNTESS

"*D ove sono . . .*" questioned the dulcet, plangent voice of Emily Nissaki at the beginning of the third act of *The Marriage of Figaro*. And "Where indeed are they, those previous happy moments?" silently echoed Leila Hopper from the third row of the stalls.

"*Dove andaro i giuramenti . . .*" sang the handsome black-haired American soprano, in the role she was rapidly making her own. And: "Too right, where have they gone, those vows of a deceiving tongue?" recited Leila bitterly to herself. She felt at that moment that she had all too much in common with the Countess Almaviva since both of them faced a predicament caused, essentially, by an unfaithful man.

"Oh heavens! To what humiliation am I reduced by a cruel husband!": those words also had found a tragic echo in Leila Hopper's heart. Except that Leila intended to deal with her own off-stage predicament rather differently. No masquerade for her, no changing clothes with her maid—

what maid? Leila didn't have a maid—and above all no sweet reconciliation at the end of the day.

"*Più docile io sono* . . ." Yes, the forgiving Countess on stage was going to be a good deal kinder to her husband than Leila was going to be to Charlie Hopper. For what Leila had in mind was murder.

Not the murder of Charlie himself however: reared on the fine old tradition of operatic vengeance, Leila planned something subtler, crueller and finally, she hoped, more devastating. For Leila intended that at the post-opera party in the theatre bar—a party for the theatre's patrons— Charlie should personally administer poison to his mistress. Not for nothing had Leila thrilled to the macabre and tragic plight of Rigoletto, convinced the wayward Duke was inside the sack which actually contained the body of his daughter. And then there were the twists of the plot of *Tosca* by which the singer finally delivered her own lover's death warrant. Charlie Hopper should hand the poisoned chalice— actually the free glass of wine for the patrons—to Magdalen Belport. Thus he would always know that he personally had brought about her agonizing death.

What about Leila's own position in all this? Did she really expect to elude discovery for very long? It was true that she had persuaded Charlie in one of his good-husbandly moments to purchase the poison in question on her behalf. (A peculiarly nasty garden potion destined to reduce errant lawns to scorched earth, it was accompanied by a list of warnings which had caused Charlie to observe mildly, "What price the ecology these days, darling?" But when Leila had retorted, "If you weren't away so much and helped me more in the garden . . ." Charlie had dumped the poison and hastily changed the subject.) Since Charlie had indubitably purchased the poison, it would be Charlie's word against hers when it came to the question of who had actually administered it.

At the same time, more grandly, Leila did not expect and did not want to avoid discovery for very long for the crime of passion she was about to commit. After all, what did life hold for her, now that she had lost Charlie?

"*J'ai perdu mon Eurydice . . .*"—Leila adored Gluck— even if she was an unlikely Orpheus and Charlie, handsome broad-shouldered Charlie, an even more improbable Eurydice.

But Magdalen Belport, of all women in the world! It was not that Magdalen Belport lacked beauty. The late Earl of Belport had died childless some years ago leaving Magdalen, his fourth, much younger, wife, a large fortune and the right to queen it at Belport Park for her lifetime. Whatever his faults, he had known how to pick a woman who would in a sense grace the role of Countess. Previous countesses had been renowned for their looks in periods which stretched back into the thirties. Magdalen, a former model (as the newspapers never failed to point out), had the long legs, the narrow hips and neatly catlike features of her original profession. With her elegant, unchanging leanness—she had to be well over 40—and an endless fund of money at her disposal, Magdalen Belport could cut more dash at a patrons' function in a pair of white silk trousers and a sequinned matador's jacket than all the other women in more conventional evening dress. Leila knew. She had seen her do it . . .

No, the fearful cruelty of Charlie's behaviour lay in the relative positions of Leila Hopper and Magdalen Belport within the Festival organization. And who knew the facts of this better than Charlie himself? As Countess of Belport, by far the most glamorous local figure, Magdalen acted as titular Chairman of the Festival committee. This meant that she attended at least one committee meeting, and bought a great many tickets (some of which she always gave away, whether she attended the performance or not, since Magdalen's friends were not exactly passionate lovers of the opera). If Magdalen did attend, she could be guaranteed to behave with the utmost benevolence, glittering matador jacket and all, and make remarks which were on the whole gracefully innocuous—Magdalen liked to please. Then she always went on to accept all the credit for the work of the Festival. That was the work which had actually been carried out, dutifully, devotedly, day in, day out, or so it often seemed, by Leila Hopper.

Leila's love of opera might be verging on the obsessional—she knew in her heart of hearts that it was—but then so, she had always thought, was Charlie's own passion for the subject. And yet he had not appreciated the sheer disloyalty of an affair with Magdalen Belport. It was as though to denigrate all their shared feelings for the Festival, the pooled task of finding singers, arranging programmes, in all of which Charlie had so often said, "You *are* the Belport Festival. Don't worry about the public thank you. Magdalen Countess of B. is just our essential figurehead, a publicity-mad mermaid on the prow of our ship. A woman who actually thinks Pavarotti is a bass"—Leila had laughed at the time, much reassured by Charlie's words—"just because he's got that wonderful deep barrel-chest. No, she actually said that to me. You'd think even Magdalen noticed that wasn't exactly a bass singing 'Nessun dorma' at the time of the World Cup." And surely Charlie had laughed too.

Given Charlie's essentially lighthearted temperament, the wayward nature which Leila both loved and deplored, she had often thought that a passion for opera was the deepest, most stable thing in her husband's life. Had it not drawn them together in the first place—that magic evening at the Coliseum listening to Linda Esther Gray as Isolde? Yes, opera was Charlie's greatest passion—until his passion for Magdalen Belport, that is.

"My lovely Countess": Leila would always remember how she found out: those words overheard on the telephone when Charlie had imagined she was working late in her tiny Festival office, following immediately on the highly disquieting incident of the trip to Venice. Charlie Hopper had always travelled a great deal, mainly to America, since his work as a rather grand kind of salesman demanded it, and Leila, since she had no choice, accepted the fact. Charlie did after all in consequence get to hear of rising young stars in the States who might be prepared to visit Belport: that was part of the way in which the Festival work had drawn travelling Charlie and homebound Leila together. (Emily Nissaki, whom Charlie had heard sing Mimì while in Chicago, was an example of that kind of happy serendipity between husband and wife.)

What she did not accept, could never accept, and was now going to take violent action to end, was Charlie's new passion for Magdalen, which meant that since that Venetian trip—as it turned out to be—he had hardly seemed to cast an affectionate glance in Leila's direction, let alone a caress. No Micaela bewailing her lost happiness with Don José had ever felt more piercing sorrow than Leila recalling how long it was since Charlie last made love to her.

"Charlie Hopper! Last seen in Harry's Bar in Venice!" Odd that those seemingly innocent words of international travelling snobbery could have destroyed Leila's peace of mind for ever. It was some party at Belport Park in aid—as usual—of fund-raising for the Festival. Leila did not know the man concerned, a big man with receding brown curly hair and a well-cut suit which probably concealed rather too many years of good living. At Harry's Bar, Venice, and elsewhere.

Now Charlie had never, so far as Leila knew, been to Venice; the reason she thought she knew this was that La Fenice was one of those opera houses, described but never visited, which they had both yearned to see for themselves. The person who had been to Venice, many times, no doubt, but certainly very recently, was Magdalen Belport. In her generous way she had even brought Leila a present back— some elegant gold and glass beads. The necklace was intended, Magdalen said, as a thank you to Leila for all the hard work she had done in the run-up to the present Ballet Festival.

At the word "Ballet" Leila had felt a moment's genuine bewilderment. Surely even Magdalen . . .

But Magdalen had quickly corrected herself. "Whoops, sweetie, opera. Trills not spills. It's just that I'm on so many committees. You know the feeling."

Leila, who was on only one committee herself, smiled forgivingly and allowed Magdalen to fasten the beads around her neck. (What treachery that seemed! Leila had since smashed them to pieces.)

"Harry's Bar?" questioned Charlie; he was using his lying voice; Leila who loved him could tell immediately. "I don't get it."

But Magdalen interrupted him. Unlike Charlie, she spoke rather too fast, as if concerned to override whatever Charlie might be going to say.

"Venice!" she exclaimed. "Don't you remember? We bumped into each other. There was that vast mass of people, all making a terrible noise, a lot of Italians, well, I suppose that was hardly surprising. You were alone. I was with a large party."

"Oh, Venice," said Charlie after a pause as though he had

somehow thought the conversation to be about quite another place, New York, Boston, Chicago (to name three cities he had recently visited). He gazed steadily at Magdalen, which meant of course that he avoided looking at Leila. "Harry's Bar in *Venice*," he repeated, still staring at Magdalen with that yearning intensity.

Later that night, Leila was first of all informed by Charlie that he had only briefly visited Venice from Munich (where he also sometimes went on business *en route* from the United States) and had hardly thought it worthwhile mentioning to Leila. Then he changed his story. The truth was, he finally blurted out, after some hours of talk in which the subject never quite went away, that Magdalen Belport had asked him to escort her to an opera gala at La Fenice. She had been let down, she needed an escort—"You know what she's like"—Charlie had been in Munich, they had been in touch over some matter to do with the Festival, he had flown down. There was nothing else to it. Absolutely nothing. And now would Leila stop all this and leave him in peace?

Charlie Hopper closed the conversation at this point by going out of the room abruptly and slamming the door. But Leila saw by the light on the telephone that he went to make a call. It was a call that lasted some time. And when Charlie did come to bed, once again he turned away from his wife.

The next morning all he said was, "I thought you might be jealous. Missing out on La Fenice. You can ask Magdalen if you like. Nothing else to it."

Jealous! It hardly seemed an adequate description of her bewildered feelings. Nor did she intend to raise the subject with Magdalen Belport. It was Magdalen who raised it with her, the next morning paying one of her rare visits to the

Festival office. She used exactly the same phrase as Charlie had, Leila noticed.

"An escort, darling. Nothing else to it."

"What was it?" asked Leila suddenly and, for her, very sharply, so that Magdalen opened her slanting cat's eyes in astonishment.

"The opera!" Leila almost shouted. "What opera did you go to?"

But at this Magdalen merely smiled in her most feline lazy way. "Oh, darling, you don't expect me to remember that. That's your department. But I do know what I wore: grey satin blazer from St. Laurent, very pretty with paler grey crêpe trousers."

It was quite possible, thought Leila rather wearily, that Magdalen was actually speaking the truth.

Then: "My lovely Countess." It was those words, overheard twelve hours later, which finally convinced Leila that the unbelievable had to be believable: her adored Charlie had transferred all the passion of his nature to Magdalen Belport. And after that, of course, in a terrible brutal way, everything began to fit in. Charlie's increasingly obvious desire to please Magdalen, for example, notably during the meetings of the Festival committee. His flattery of her taste, even her taste in opera and possible singers for the Festival . . . now that was really going too far. "My lovely Countess," perhaps, but knowledgeable about opera never!

There was one peculiarly humiliating incident which actually took place in the committee. Leila was as a matter of fact used to smoothing over Magdalen's cultural gaffes—obviously not infrequent in a woman who could think Pavarotti was a bass on the grounds that he had a barrel-chest. She had brought it to a fine art—or so she thought. A quick change of subject, and a quick correction of the minutes afterwards, seemed to result in satisfaction all round.

But now Magdalen insisted that *La bohème* was the story of a fun-loving courtesan called Violetta; one who went on a glorious spree to the country with her lover, and then came back, only to die of TB in his arms. And Charlie agreed with her! Leila could hardly believe her ears. For the first time she actually contradicted Magdalen, instead of merely altering the record.

Maybe Leila's voice did rise as she began: "You are thinking of *La traviata*, for heaven's sake. Isn't she, Charlie! In *La bohème* there are these students—"

But that was no excuse for Magdalen to lean back delicately in the face of Leila's passion and confide to Charlie, "I've always identified myself with Violetta. I adore doomed people, don't you? That's why *La bohème* is absolutely my favourite *numero uno* opera." And still Charlie, Charlie of all people, did nothing.

On stage the opera was almost over and the Count, a short fat man with none of Charlie's handsome looks, was asking his wife to forgive him. "*Contessa, perdona!*"

"I am kinder: I will say yes," his wife responded in the rather better-looking incarnation of Emily Nissaki. It had always been one of the moving moments in Leila's canon of opera. No longer. For Charlie Hopper (and Magdalen Belport) there was to be no forgiveness. Doomed people: yes, indeed. In a very short time the post-opera party would begin in the theatre bar. And a very short time after that Magdalen, Countess of Belport, would be dead.

How convenient that Leila, as secretary of the committee, generally looked after the doling out of the patrons' free drink! It was with special care that Leila handed the fatal glass to Charlie in order that he might—equally fatally—pass it on.

"I've got something special for her. She really wants champagne, of course. But this is at least better than the usual plonk. Take it to her."

Then Leila could not resist adding—what madness overtook her when she had held her tongue for so long?—"Take it to your lovely Countess."

For a moment Charlie, now holding the glass, stood staring at Leila. His expression was one of total amazement, followed almost immediately by guilt.

"She knows." That was what his expression said to her, as clear as words. "She's known all the time."

Leila's own expression, which had been momentarily triumphant, changed to blandness.

"Go on, darling, give it to her." It was her usual polite, affectionate tone, the tone of an organizer who needs to make everyone happy. "*Figaro* is not exactly short. She must need it."

"She must indeed," replied Charlie levelly, the amazement and the guilt by now well concealed. He turned away. Leila followed the direction of his tall, black-dinner-jacketed figure, that formal guise which set off his fair English good looks to perfection. She watched Charlie edging his way through the crowd, polite, skilful, not spilling a drop. There he went, remorselessly towards the corner where Magdalen Belport, svelte as ever in one of her embroidered jackets which surely came direct from Christian Lacroix, held court. Despite the crowd which surrounded her, Magdalen Belport looked up to give Charlie a special intimate smile. Leila watched Charlie, holding her breath. Now, now, let him hold out the glass, let him perhaps kiss her on the cheek—for the last time—but let him at least hold out the glass, let his be the hand, let her drink from it—

But wait— No, for God's sake—

"No!" screamed Leila involuntarily. She stopped. "No, Charlie, no," she wanted to cry. "Not her . . ."

It was too late. Already the wine was coursing down the throat of Emily Nissaki, that pampered throat soon to be closed and silent for ever in death, as she flung back her handsome head with its abundant coils of dark hair, the relic of her Greek ancestry, smiling her thanks with her bold black sloe eyes fixed on Charlie Hopper who had handed her the drink.

Beside her, Magdalen, Countess of Belport, wondered when Charlie Hopper, or at least that hard-working, opera-mad wife of his, would bother to bring her a drink. After all she was the Chairman of the Festival. Hadn't there been something about a special glass of wine? Yet Leila had been behaving so curiously lately, sulking really, she who had always been so grateful for everything. Could she possibly have found out about Charlie . . . Magdalen hoped to God she wasn't planning to leave the Festival office or anything drastic like that. Leila was so clever, so inventive.

So when was that special glass of wine coming? The plonk in the theatre bar was famously disgusting, poisonous one might almost say, even if that face the lead singer was now pulling was surely slightly over the top even for a dramatic soprano.

The death of Emily Nissaki, popularly described as being on stage—the theatre bar was surely near enough to count as that—created a predictable sensation. There were those, it is true, who suggested that her macabre ending cast a false retrospective glamour on her actual talent. But then none of those critics had probably heard her sing in person: those few records so far released did not quite do her justice.

These same critics had not, for example, as Charlie Hopper had done, ecstatically followed Emily Nissaki round American opera houses—and to Venice—throughout her brief career; following that first *coup de foudre* meeting with her in Chicago.

Finally Charlie had secured, with some quiet manipulation, that "my lovely Countess" as he was wont to call her—a reference to that glorious night together following her performance in *Figaro* at La Fenice—should come to the Belport Festival. (Even if it had involved flattery beyond the call of duty to Magdalen Belport: still remarkable looking, if you like, and a good sort, but altogether too fond of making men into slaves. If Charlie was going to be a slave, it would be to an opera singer like Emily Nissaki, not to an idle rich woman.)

To the rest of the spectators, the way in which Leila Hopper, shortly before confessing her crime, cried out, "The wrong Countess!" made no sense. She then quoted the general exclamation at the end of *Figaro* of "Heavens! What do I see?" "The wrong Countess!": what could that mean? She had known, surely she had known, of Charlie's affair with Emily Nissaki—otherwise why poison her?

She must have known. It was Magdalen Belport for example who reported seeing Emily Nissaki and Charlie Hopper together in Venice.

"Not that I told Leila," Magdalen added quickly. "In fact after Geoffrey's gaffe I tried like mad to cover up for Charlie by pretending he was alone; whereas of course he was hanging round the neck of that wretched singer, Emily Whatnot. And then I backed him up with Leila to the hilt. Some cock and bull story about going to the opera. As if one didn't have better things to do in Venice! Absolutely to the hilt."

It was only Charlie himself, broken not only by the death

of Emily but also by the part he had unwittingly played in it, who knew exactly what his wife had meant by her frantic cry of "The wrong Countess!" And her use of those words from *Figaro* confirmed it to him. "Heavens! What do I see?" exclaimed all those on stage when the "right" Countess finally stepped out of the alcove to reveal herself. (Not that he could ever tell Magdalen Belport, unaware both of Leila's suspicions and of the peril which had threatened her.)

"Take it to your lovely Countess": how could Charlie have looked in any other direction than towards Emily Nissaki? And so in a sense Leila Hopper, self-confessed murderess Leila, did have her operatic revenge.

9
THE TWIST

Something about the way the woman twisted her rings, took one off, swapped it round with another, transferred rings from finger to finger, hand to hand, surveyed the result and then began the nervous twisting all over again, reminded me of Margaret. But these rings, so far as I could see, were not the gleaming diamond clusters, glinting ruby half-hoops, heavy sapphire globules with which Margaret had been wont to play. These were plain white rings, ivory rings at best, but more likely plastic, gold rings which were so clearly not made of precious metal that they reminded one disagreeably of curtain rings.

The woman opposite me in the carriage continued to twist her rings. In that nervously repeated gesture was all the resemblance: for one thing this woman looked far older than Margaret must be now, last seen in all her pampered glory of fur and silk. However Margaret had aged—and she must of course have aged to some degree over the intervening years—she would have managed to age gracefully. And she could never have aged *downhill* as it were. I knew exactly the kind of old—or rather middle-aged—woman Margaret would have become; you see them sometimes at parties, fragile, elegant and protected, still candles for all the male moths while the younger beauties sulk at their unexpected neglect. This woman, in a blackish overcoat and dirty boots, was near to a tramp: what was more, there were bruises on her face.

Then I looked again, at the woman still twisting her shoddy rings. I looked again and saw that the woman was Margaret. Margaret, my ex-wife.

I will not deny that I experienced one short, savage pang of sheer pleasure. After that pity and pity alone overwhelmed me. Had Margaret remained as svelte and beautiful as she had been under my besotted care, I should certainly have felt very differently, experiencing neither the pleasure nor the pity. I might have felt a brief stab of pain for the past on first sighting her; after that I would have tried to escape from the encounter. Certainly I should have tried to escape if she had been accompanied by Jason.

Jason: her second husband and my ex-partner, as I suppose I must call him. But I have never seen either of them following the divorce, I took care of that, and perhaps they did too; so to me he is still in my thoughts Jason, her lover and my partner. Just as she is still, somewhere in my thoughts, still Margaret, my Margaret and my wife. It was that thought which provoked the pity, that and her total physical degradation.

The bruises—who? Surely Jason was not responsible. I had accused my partner—my ex-partner—of many things in my mind over the last twenty years, but violence or even a tendency towards violence was not amongst them. As for poverty, our business affairs were no longer linked as they had been, but even I knew enough to realize that Jason must remain an extremely rich man. Besides, this Margaret at whom I was gazing with pity was not only poor but had evidently been poor for some years. No sudden fall from wealth would account for the haggard, battered face, the cast-off clothing.

At that moment, Margaret looked up. Her eyes, her once beautiful eyes, met mine. To my horror, I found that my own filled with tears. But Margaret herself gazed back without expression, merely continuing that twisting, that eternal twisting of the rings.

"Meg," I said.

The woman, Margaret, said nothing in reply; her gaze was in fact quite vacant as though she had not recognized me. Of course I had not recognized *her* at first. But then I, I am well preserved. Everyone says so. I have taken care of myself (having no one to take care of me). Or perhaps it would be more realistic to admit that I have always looked much as I do now, which is staid, middle-aged, and respectable. "Darling, you look like a man of 60 already," had been one of Margaret's favourite jibes. "Why can't you go to a better tailor?" After a bit, I realized that this meant: why can't you go to Jason's tailor? And I stopped my pathetic, earnest attempts to please her sartorially. I think that cruel moment was when I knew that Margaret was going to leave me.

I stood up and crossed the carriage. I touched the woman on the shoulder.

"Margaret," I said. "It's me, Andrew."

Margaret looked up at me; her fingers at the rings were suddenly still. Then I saw the white stick lying beside her, previously hidden by her black coat.

"Andrew?" she said rather doubtfully. "I thought I recognized your voice just now. But sometimes one hears voices. You know how it is." Then with more energy she added, "You *don't* know how it is."

"Meg," I said tenderly, finding all the familiar protective yearning come back to me.

"Oh, Andrew," she cried suddenly, feeling up towards my arm and anchoring her hand upon it. "Andrew, help me." It was a voice of pleading and need that she had never used in all the years of our marriage, the teasing, critical Margaret gone for ever. "Please will you help me? You don't know what happened to me—"

There and then in the carriage, I kissed her, stopped her speaking with my gentle kiss. There would be time for her to tell me these things. I held her bruised face in mine, marking how old she looked, the skin lined, the hair listless, and touched the hands adorned with their cheap rings, which had brought her back to me.

Her hands! The state of her hands alone chilled me when I thought of my Margaret's soft white hands and pearly nails, hands which belonged as much to her manicurist (as I once lightly told her) as they did to me. I do not know what I would have done then. Taken her home, bathed her, kissed her again many times, always gently, to show that I could overlook the loss of her beauty, cared for her—

But at that point I found myself waking from this dream, this delicious dream (for it was certainly no nightmare). And I felt the warm hand of my wife Margaret, lying beside me on the pillow between us in our bed. I could feel the nobbles and sharpness of her rings, the many rings which she never took off, even at night. I would like to have wrenched off those rings from her fingers, before I killed her, twisting her own silk scarf round her neck, twisting it many times as she herself was wont to twist her jewellery. I would like her to have lain dead there with curtain rings and cheap plastic on her beautiful fingers.

But there was no time. So I killed her as she lay, still in her jewels, I killed her for her treachery and her adultery and her mockery and her twisting, twisting fingers which even in death would not give up their sparkling secrets. Margaret, now my dead wife.

ABOUT THE AUTHOR

ANTONIA FRASER's seven previous mysteries featuring Jemima Shore—the latest is *The Cavalier Case*—have been translated into many languages, as has her previous collection of short stories, *Jemima Shore's First Case*. They have also inspired two television series, *Quiet as a Nun* with Maria Aitken and *Jemima Shore Investigates* starring Patricia Hodge. Antonia Fraser is well known as a biographer, was President of English PEN from 1988–89, and is also a past Chairman of both the Society of Authors and the Crimewriters' Association.